A MATTER OF INHERITANCE

Margaret Stewart Taylor

CHIVERS·PRESS·BATH

First published in Great Britain 1983
by
Robert Hale Limited
This Large Print edition published by
Chivers Press
by arrangement with
Robert Hale Limited
1992

ISBN 0 7451 5564 2

British Library Cataloguing in Publication Data available

CE

father,
ge to an
phaned
s to her
and is
she has
visit the
ay their
should
for her
Leonin,
e of the
ttracted
e is no

A MATTER OF INHERITANCE

CHAPTER ONE

Valerie leant back against the swabs of the travelling coach hired by her aunt to complete their journey from London to Vienna.

Yes, it looked a beautiful city full of fine buildings, but Valerie was in no mood to appreciate the beauty. She was secretly vexed about delay there when her interest was centred on Karpathy Castle in eastern Hungary.

How would the grandfather she had never seen receive her? He had only learnt of her existence a few weeks ago, yet immediately he sent Aunt Irma to London for her.

Valerie glanced at this newly-acquired relative sitting beside her. Mama had never mentioned an elder sister, only a brother Julius who made a suitably aristocratic marriage which soon produced a son. His child Leonin was four years old when Valerie's mother eloped with John Gilliott, thereby incurring Count Karpathy's wrath, a wrath so fierce that he cast off his daughter Lilla.

Not before she was fourteen did Valerie persuade her mother to tell her the full story. Lilla grudgingly acknowledged, 'I suppose you ought to know, darling, but promise me to say nothing to your father. My father's behaviour to him was a cruel blow to his pride, and you

1

know what a sensitive man he is.'

John Gilliott had inherited a fortune made by his forebears through trade. He had been brought up to assume this wealth would more than compensate for his being of lowly stock, the descendant of traders, not landed gentry. There was no need for him to earn a living, and as he had great curiosity to see countries other than his own he travelled widely and eventually came to Hungary. He carried a general letter of introduction from the English ambassador, so when he reached Karpathy Castle he was graciously received by the Count. Hungarian nobles deemed hospitality a duty imposed upon their rank, but this particular situation changed when the guest fell in love with Countess Lilla and asked for her hand in marriage. It was unthinkable, declared Count Karpathy, that his daughter should wed a man of humble birth. As for being the son of a wealthy London merchant, it would have been almost as shameful if he had been the son of a Jewish moneylender. The latter were plentiful in Hungary. That country's nobility was frequently getting into debt.

'My father was an intolerant autocrat,' went on Lilla. 'If I had not loved John so deeply I dared not have disobeyed the order never to see him again. We had no choice but to run away secretly, marry, and come to England. My father did not pursue us. As far as I was concerned I had ceased to be his daughter, so I never wrote, not even to tell him of your birth. Now I have satisfied your curiosity, Valerie, you must not hurt Papa by letting him know I have confided in you.'

'I promise, Mama,' said Valerie.

She loved her father too dearly to cause him pain.

John Gilliott was a loving husband and parent. He was good-looking, very charming, but hopelessly extravagant and impractical. He had grown up believing the fortune he inherited had no limits, so when doubly orphaned at seventeen, Valerie found herself completely penniless. The grand country house in Leicestershire and the fashionable mansion in London, with contents, were claimed by creditors. Papa had no near relatives, and she wanted nothing to do with the Hungarian family from which her mother had been banished.

I must earn my own living, she declared to herself though with little conviction.

Advised by the attorney, Valerie registered with an agency, had difficulty in obtaining a post but at last became governess to four detestably spoilt children, aged five to ten. Lack of qualifications and experience enabled Mrs Pearson to declare that keep and a few pounds a year was all the salary Miss Gilliott could expect. Valerie had no alternative but to accept.

3

Several months of misery followed. Then, with pride shattered and a conviction that neither of her dead parents would wish her to continue in this unhappy state, she wrote to Count Karpathy, Karpathy Castle, Hungary, appealing for financial help so that she could leave the Pearsons and live in London while she tried to obtain a companion's post. It was a dreadful thing to do, especially when Papa had been so insulted by the Count, but it was the course of action the family attorney had originally advised. She scorned it then. Now she found the Pearson ménage so impossible she did not care what she did to escape from the misery of working there. Papa and Mama would have understood. As for the grandfather refusing to help, fortunately that did not occur to Valerie.

It was a glorious moment when she was summoned to the withdrawing-room and greeted as 'my dear niece' by an elegantly dressed, haughty lady, who announced she had been sent by the Count Karpathy to conduct Valerie to Hungary. And there was hard, plump Mrs Pearson gasping with awe...

Driving through Vienna, Valerie was about to savour that scene for the hundredth time when Aunt Irma, otherwise Frau von Moricz, directed her attention to an imposing building on the left.

'That is the Metternich Palace, niece.'

'Metternich Palace?' Valerie was obviously bewildered.

'The town palace of Prince Metternich. He is a close friend of mine and, for my sake, obtained an important government post for Hugo.'

Hugo was Aunt Irma's only child. Valerie enquired who was this Prince Metternich, and the aunt gave an impatient gasp at such ignorance.

'He is our great statesman, the one who really rules Austria and her dependencies. The Emperor is ... er ... rather a weak personage. Prince Metternich directed peace settlements after the defeat of that Corsican ogre Napoleon. Surely you have heard of the Congress of Vienna?'

'But it is history, Aunt. It happened more than thirty years ago. I was not born then.'

'Oh, the Prince is the full threescore and ten now, but his brain is as agile as men far younger, and he is still the virtual ruler of Austria—and of course, Hungary.'

'But Hungary is a separate country, although its king happens to be Austrian Emperor as well.'

Valerie's mother had said very little about her homeland, but she had mentioned that fact. Repeated now, the effect on Aunt Irma was a declaration that the title King of Hungary meant nothing. Hungary was subordinate to

Austria and ruled by her emperors.

'Mama said Hungarians were a different race, mostly Magyars as she was.'

'Noble families like the Karpathys are intensely loyal to the present Emperor. Yes, we are Magyars with a different language, but it is only used among peasants. Normally we speak German.'

'I am glad,' said Valerie. 'Mama never taught me the Magyar tongue.'

She did not add that use of it would probably have vexed her father, whose wounded pride after Count Karpathy's insults made him ignore his wife's past life. Valerie remembered him looking furious when a visitor called Lilla a Hungarian countess. That incident roused Valerie's curiosity and eventually she asked her mother the truth, but was only told on condition she did not distress her father by any reference to it.

Aunt Irma was talking scornfully of peasants in Hungary who paid attention to nonsense talked by agitators, although their noble lords tried to stamp out dangerous ideas.

Further conversation was prevented by the coach stopping in front of a tall narrow house with a distinctive look of elegance about it. A groom sitting beside the driver jumped down, used with force the brass knocker on the front door, then opened the vehicle's door for Frau von Moricz and Valerie to alight.

They had just reached the top of the three front steps when the house door was opened by a manservant in green and silver livery. As if summoned by magic, two men hurried to remove baggage and carry it indoors by a side entrance. Valerie followed her aunt into a hall where two lines of servants were waiting to pay their respects to the returning mistress. As she had done repeatedly during their journey, Valerie contrasted the behaviour of her aunt with that of her mother. It seemed impossible the two were sisters.

Aunt Irma had confessed to being several years older than Mama, the youngest child, and their brother Julius. He had married the daughter of a Russian nobleman. Mama remembered her, her death, and the son she bore, Leonin, who was four when Mama eloped. Therefore Valerie calculated he must be five years her senior.

During the journey to Vienna she had learnt that Uncle Julius was killed during a boar hunt, and now it was assumed that Leonin, heir to Karpathy, had perished somewhere in Russia on his way back from a visit to St Petersburg.

'Nothing has been heard of him for two years, so he must be dead. Yet my poor father refuses to face that reality.'

'Is Russia a dangerous country?' asked Valerie.

'Extremely dangerous! A terrible country!

My hubsand went there once and hated it. Naturally Leonin would have had servants accompanying him, but anything could happen, like an attack by wolves or by robbers. His mother's family has made full enquiries, and they are influential people, standing high in the Tsar's favour. If they can discover nothing, then the worst must have happened. I believe Leonin to be dead. He was heir to the Karpathy estates and title, but if the direct male line is extinct, then my father has power to leave everything to me because I am the eldest daughter. After me, Hugo will inherit.'

In travelling coaches and on the steam packet-boat, Valerie had heard praise of Hugo sung by his doting mother. Aunt Irma was a widow and he was her only child. It seemed strange, thought Valerie, that Mama had never mentioned a sister while she spoke of the existence of Julius, and Julius's son. Valerie had the feeling of entering a completely strange world. Meeting the formidable grandfather was the most terrifying ordeal that lay ahead. Aunt Irma was not taking her straight to Hungary, as apparently Hugo was not able to leave Vienna immediately.

She was certainly bored to hear so constantly about him and his shining qualities. He was handsome, popular, a paragon of all virtues, and highly esteemed by all, including Prince Metternich.

8

'The dear boy is twenty-eight.'

'Ten years older than me.'

'But you won't find that any obstacle to friendship,' and Aunt Irma gave a tinkling laugh, its meaning lost on the unsuspicious Valerie.

'He will take you riding in the Prater.'

'Is the Prater near Karpathy Castle?'

'Good heavens, child! The Prater is in Vienna. It used to be a private imperial hunting ground, but is now open to the public. There are fine avenues through the trees where people ride.'

'Surely we shall not be long in Vienna, Aunt. My grandfather sent you with great haste to fetch me.'

'Only because he felt it shocking for a girl with Karpathy blood in her veins to be acting as governess. Earning her living, like a common peasant! My dear, you are nobility—well partly so—and you must behave as such.'

A crushed Valerie asked about riding in Hungary.

'Oh, everyone rides there. Karpathy Castle lies by an immense plain called the Alfold. Didn't your mother describe the country?'

'No, she did not talk about her old home, so I have no clear idea what to expect. Tell me more about my grandfather. Does he really want to see me?'

'Yes, but you realise he cannot forget your

mother's disgraceful behaviour in marrying against his wishes.'

'Mama was in love.'

Irma von Moricz shrugged her shoulders at this remark. She went on to say, 'He instructed me to notify him by letter as soon as we reached Vienna, and I shall do so the evening we arrive.'

At last they had arrived, and Valerie was aghast at the way her aunt ignored the bows and bobs of the waiting servants. Her mother would have been gracious and smiling, and Mama was equally well-born. In those far-off days before she died and Papa found he had lost all his money and shot himself in despair, Valerie recalled returns to the Grange and the town house. They were happy and the faithful servants were happy.

Not here, for Frau von Moricz swept past as if servants were as inanimate as the costly rugs strewn on the marble floor. She led her niece upstairs.

'You shall see the entertaining rooms later. Besides eating-room and withdrawing-room, there is a thirty foot salon where I give parties, or hold musical concerts. Now this is your bedchamber.'

It was a floor higher and at the back of the house, but vastly superior to the cramped apartment allotted to Mrs Pearson's governess. Magda, Aunt Irma's personal maid, brought in Valerie's small amount of baggage and

10

proceeded quickly to unpack.

'I cannot spare Magda to attend to your toilette.'

'That would be quite unnecessary, Aunt. I am used to managing for myself. I am afraid I have only the one dinner gown.'

'Yes, I have noticed the poor state of your wardrobe, and I must see about you having proper outfits for all occasions before you can appear before my friends. There will be no guests this evening.'

'Just you and me, Aunt Irma?'

'Hugo will be with us, of course.'

Then followed instructions about Valerie presenting herself in the withdrawing-room when she heard the dinner gong.

Left alone, Valerie washed and dressed with the speed to which she had become accustomed as the Pearson governess. Then she sat wondering what her cousin Hugo would be like, and, what was more important, the grandfather who sounded so frightening. She really was apprehensive about the future and wondered if she had done the right thing in writing to Karpathy Castle, but anything must be better than acting as governess to those horrible Pearson children. She laughed at the memory of Mrs Pearson's cringing behaviour to Aunt Irma on learning the downtrodden, underpaid governess was the granddaughter of a Hungarian count.

Time dragged on. If only she had a book to read. Perhaps there was a bookroom near the withdrawing-room where she was to go at the sound of the gong. Valerie thought she might also peep at the salon where musical parties were held.

Corridor, staircase, and hall were ablaze with light, but nobody was about. No door she opened revealed a bookroom, and then she found herself in what was obviously the salon. Darkness had fallen and there was no artificial light here, but the heavy blue silk curtains were not drawn across the long windows, so moonlight streamed through the glass. Avoiding a grand piano, she went towards a window and looked down on the street. The curtains were so soft and rich that it was impossible not to put her cheek against the material in sensuous enjoyment. Aunt Irma was going to buy her new outfits and Valerie thought how she would revel in a gown of similar luxurious silk. She drew closer to the window and wrapped a curtain fold around her. Then she began to watch people passing the house, some on foot, some driving along the road. They all looked prosperous, but this was clearly a fashionable district. Valerie suspected there was also a Vienna of slums and artisans.

I wonder what Hungary will be like.

Suddenly she was shocked by her ignorance of that land. She did not even know if there

12

were any large towns. Aunt Irma had said that Karpathy Castle was near a huge plain called the Alfold.

At this point the door opened and she was conscious that two people had entered the salon. They did not come far into the room, but after one had taken the precaution of shutting the door they stood talking in the semi-darkness. Huddled in the curtain by a window, Valerie was not visible, nor dare she venture to peep at them. She heard a man's voice uttering terms of endearment, a woman responding with appreciative giggles, and the unmistakable sound of noisy kisses.

'More! More!'

'You are a hot little bitch, Kataya. Oh, I wish I could enjoy you immediately, but you know I have to dine with Mother and this nuisance of a cousin.'

'Why has Frau von Moricz brought the creature from England?'

There was no direct reply but the man said,

'Mother will be furious if she discovers you did not return to Hesse as she ordered.'

'You promised to look after me.'

'Oh, I'll find you somewhere to hide in Vienna now she is back here, only remember I pay for sole rights. Don't think you can make money on the side by sharing your favours with other men.'

'You know you can trust me.'

'I know perfectly well I cannot. Now make yourself scarce until midnight when you are to come to the back door and Adolph will be there to let you in, and bring you to my chamber. Mother will have retired to bed by then. It will be too dangerous for that to happen again so I have told Adolph to hire an apartment where I can visit you.'

'Shall I have to stay there all the time? How dull!'

'Those are the terms for my protection. Now you must leave. Slip out carefully and don't let anyone see you.'

'Give me a little pleasure first, Hugo. You know how crazy I am about you.'

'There isn't time. Dinner will be served in half an hour. Not that I shall want any food when I am starving for your body. God, I don't know when any woman has excited me like you do!'

The listening Valerie gasped. Was this the way lovers talked in real life? It was vastly different from what heroes and heroines did in the few romantic novels Mama had allowed her to read.

There were more sounds of kissing. Then the door opened, letting in a shaft of light from outside. The newcomer was Aunt Irma. Valerie recognised her angry voice.

'What is the meaning of this? I dismissed you and ordered you to return to Hesse.'

14

A string of abusive epithets against the girl followed. From their first meeting at Mrs Pearson's, Valerie had instinctively disliked Aunt Irma, although Mama's sister and emissary of Count Karpathy, sent by him to rescue her from a life that offered nothing but a succession of governess and companion posts, or sheer starvation. Alternatives like prostitution were outside the range of Valerie's comprehension, as were possible stage or shop employment. She had been brought up to take her place in the fashionable world as befitted the daughter of a rich man and aristocratic mother.

With her parents' death, and without money, she was bewildered. The arrival of Aunt Irma seemed like a lifesaving raft to save her from a troubled sea. She took to it, thankful to both grandfather and aunt, eager to like and be liked. The aunt she speedily found unlovable, a fact she did her best to ignore until the present moment.

The abusive words uttered by Aunt Irma made Valerie shudder. This time the girl Kataya would be compelled to return to Hesse in a conveyance provided by her late employer.

'I shall give the driver full instructions. Then if you return to Vienna, I shall see you are put in prison, and I have the necessary influence for that to be done.'

'I say, Mother,' came Hugo's weak protest.

15

'You will spend tonight here under the guard of my housekeeper who won't stand any nonsense. Ring for Magda, Hugo. She can conduct this trollop to Holstein's room. I shall give detailed instructions later, but I want to talk to you first.'

'Scold and nag me—I know!'

'Be quiet!'

There was no escape for Valerie. Hoping she would not be discovered, she tried to shrink further into her hiding place. How she despised this unknown cousin Hugo for not defending the girl he had been making love to! Magda came and took Kataya away. Hugo turned scornfully on his mother.

'So you still have that dreary maid you engaged after getting rid of Kataya.'

'Whom I dismissed because you could not keep your hands off her.'

'I was only amusing myself, something I certainly could not do with plain, elderly Magda.'

'Never mind about my personal maids. You must keep off flirtations, society and other, while you undertake wooing of Valerie.'

'Why all the hurry, Mother? Give me time to get used to the idea of being fettered.'

'You have had plenty of time to become accustomed to my plan, and it is nonsense to talk as if you were losing your freedom. Once married you can seduce servant girls, or

16

anything else you want.'

'Keeping up my reputation of being Vienna's foremost flirt, and of course ignoring my wife's tears.'

'A wife who has any sense does not interfere with her husband's affairs.'

'You took care my father did not have any, didn't you? You were the one who held the reins, or rather the purse-strings.'

'Don't be silly, Hugo. Valerie is quite pretty. She is like Lilla in looks with golden-brown hair and the Karpathy grey eyes.'

'Unlike you, Mother. What was my maternal grandmother's colouring?'

Aunt Irma's voice betrayed irritation, but she did not contradict her son when he added that she was no Karpathy in looks. All she said was that Valerie was the type of female whom men would find attractive.

'Must have been a disadvantage when she was a governess.'

'I tell you, Hugo, you will like her. You must like her.'

'I do not wish to marry.'

'But marriage with her is important—and urgent.'

'Supposing Leonin turns up after all.'

'That is impossible.'

'Convicts sometimes escape from Siberia.'

'Very seldom, and it would be impossible to get out of the country. The Prince says Russian frontiers are strictly guarded, that there are secret police everywhere, and a passport would be demanded if the person roused suspicion. Because Leonin was condemned as a traitor his mother's relatives would not dare to help him if he did get free and seek assistance from them.'

'You certainly arranged matters cleverly with Prince Metternich's help. All the same, it is unfortunate you cannot produce your nephew's corpse, my dear Mother, since Grandfather clings to the belief Leonin is alive.'

'Absurd after two years without word of him. Father will come to his senses soon.'

'I wonder. He does not know Leonin was arrested in Russia and sent to Siberia on a charge of treason.'

'I have told him again and again that Leonin must have met with a fatal accident when travelling back to Hungary.'

'And Grandfather only declares that the Almighty would not permit the last of the Karpathy male stock to be wiped out. You'll see, he will die before he signs the will Tamas Szerb has artfully drawn up.'

'Obstinate old man! He will accept the fact of Leonin's death in time, but your position must be unassailable.'

'Supposing he dies first.'

'Die! He is still as strong as a horse and will go on a few years longer. He has never had an illness in his life. Only, Hugo, you cannot

18

afford to waste any time in winning Valerie's affections. Ignore other women and concentrate on her. Like your Aunt Lilla she is romantically inclined, so it is important to make her imagine you love her. Then she will be attracted to you.'

'Oh, Mother, did you ever meet a female who was not enraptured by my looks and charm? I am sorry she is half-English, for I have always heard the English are a cold lot.'

'Remember she is half-Magyar. Now start being attentive this very evening. You must, Hugo.'

'Before then you will have abused that poor Kataya.'

Hugo's voice died away as he followed his mother out of the salon and shut the door, leaving a stunned Valerie to digest the startling information she had acquired through eavesdropping.

Aunt Irma is planning a marriage for me with her son. But why? We have not met yet. There is no question of affection, yet her motives cannot be mercenary when I have neither money nor estates.

Valerie spoke aloud and the sound of her voice roused her to consider the immediate situation. She must not be discovered in the salon. It was imperative she got back to her bedchamber without being seen. Fortunately she managed to achieve this and sat in privacy there, trying to recall all she had learnt about

19

her cousin Hugo, mostly from his own lips in addition to what Aunt Irma revealed.

So he intended to lure her into marriage, the sole reason being that his mother wished it. Once married he would pursue other women as much as he pleased.

And those extraordinary facts about her other cousin! It seemed impossible that Leonin could be a prisoner in Siberia and that he was the victim of Aunt Irma's plotting—plotting and its result both kept secret from old Count Karpathy.

Valerie's mind was in a whirl, and when the dinner gong rang she did not hurry to leave her chamber but sat trying to adjust her mind to this fantastic situation. All along she had disliked her aunt, and now the dislike was a mixture of disgust and horror. No wonder Mama never spoke of an elder sister.

But I must behave towards Aunt Irma as if I had no notion of her real character, Valerie resolved.

Yes, she must go down to the withdrawing-room, face her aunt, and meet the flirtatious Hugo, a man whose mother determined he should marry her. And there was no proper reason for the marriage.

CHAPTER TWO

There was no doubt about it. Hugo von Moricz was all his mother claimed in physical appearance. Valerie was compelled to admit this to herself when she entered the withdrawing-room and saw him for the first time.

Aunt Irma declared, 'Here she is, Hugo.'

The tone of voice was playful but had an artificial ring. After the recently overheard conversation it strained Valerie's self-command to look unconcerned. Only Hugo's easy assurance helped.

'So you are the cousin I have heard so much about. I have been nearly consumed by impatience to meet you.'

He gave the impression she had been continually in his thoughts ever since her existence became known to him, and had it not been for the words recently exchanged between him and his mother, as well as with the dismissed maid, Valerie felt she might have succumbed to this flattery. As it was she replied in somewhat airy fashion that his mother had talked a good deal about him.

At the same time she was studying Hugo's face. He was very good-looking. His features were regular, his blue eyes lively, and a strong vitality seemed to bubble out of him. He made her think of a swift splashing fountain.

Yes, she would have been charmed by this cousin and eager to be on friendly terms if she did not already know him to be false. Those eyes danced gleefully, but the expression was assumed, and those thin lips were unpleasantly purposeful.

'I expect Mother has given you quite a wrong idea of me.'

'How?'

'Made out I am very wonderful, so you will be disappointed when you get to know me properly, Cousin Valerie.'

'I don't expect I shall,' she lied, vexed that she was unable to think of a witty response.

During the last term spent at an expensive boarding-school, Valerie had considered herself to be quite sophisticated. She was on the threshold of womanhood and about to take her place in society, but Mama became ill and died, Papa died, and all personality seemed drained out of her during that awful governess period. Now she was among relatives, but a stranger among strangers.

The three went into what Aunt Irma called the eating-room and sat down to an elaborate meal served with great pomp. Hugo started to ask questions about the journey from England, expressing sympathy for the boredom and discomforts Valerie must have endured, and when she said she had not suffered at all he announced he was no lover of travel. He then talked about Vienna and the pleasures afforded by that city. Valerie's attention was fixed on her aunt's slightly nervous expression. She must be afraid her son was sounding frivolous in emphasising these enjoyments.

Aunt Irma is so anxious for him to make a good impression on me. If I had not overheard the two in the salon, I could not believe she had such ridiculous plans for me. Surely she wants him to marry better than to a penniless cousin.

Hugo probably had no need of a wife with dowry, thought Valerie, as she listened to her aunt speaking about the important post he held directly under Prince Metternich, and how valuable and confidential was his work. No details were given and an irritated Valerie asked if old Count Karpathy approved.

'Why should he not?'

'You said Grandfather was shocked at my earning a living.'

'Ladies do not earn livings,' came her aunt's stern pronouncement. 'And for a Karpathy to be a mere governess!'

'You must have hated such degradation, Cousin Valerie.'

'I did, and that is why I wrote to the Count, only I merely asked for financial support while I trained for something better. It was a great surprise when your mother arrived in London to bring me to Hungary. How long are we to

23

stay in Vienna?'

'I have work on hand I am not free to leave yet,' said Hugo. 'Anyway, I am sure you are in no hurry to bury yourself in the country. My old grandfather is absorbed in his estates and never leaves Karpathy, but when I inherit I shall leave management of the peasants to an overseer and spend the greater part of each year in Vienna. You will understand that, Valerie, when you experience the gaieties here.'

'You say you will inherit the title?'

'Mother will when Grandfather dies and she intends to stand aside for me. He is quite old so not many years should elapse before I am Count Karpathy.'

'How can you be sure you ever will be?' demanded Valerie. 'Surely my Cousin Leonin takes precedence of Aunt Irma and you.'

'Leonin is dead.'

'I thought he was only missing.'

'Only missing! Lost somewhere in that wilderness of a country called Russia! Nothing has been heard of him for two years so he cannot possibly be alive.'

'We have made innumerable enquiries,' broke in Aunt Irma. 'Of course Leonin has perished. Torn to pieces by wolves, I expect. He probably travelled with too small an escort. His notion was to explore as he made his way south. Foolish, rash boy!'

Valerie flushed as she remembered what she

24

had heard when standing by the salon window. Afraid of betraying any clue to her eavesdropping she asked again about the anticipated letter from Count Karpathy concerning her going to Hungary.

'I have written,' declared Aunt Irma rigidly. 'There is also the matter of Prince Metternich sparing Hugo.'

'And he must come with us, must he, Aunt?'

'Of course, niece!'

Valerie longed to reply that Hugo did not seem to care much for the estates he expected to inherit, but she tactfully held her tongue, turned to him and asked for a description of the Hungarian country near Karpathy.

'I understand there will be plenty of opportunity for horse riding.'

Hugo merely replied, 'You can ride daily in the Prater here while mild weather lasts. When winter sets in I'll take you skating instead.'

Conversation for the rest of the evening turned on certain social events like balls, soirées, and musical parties. Hugo kept making facetious jokes. Aunt Irma boasted of her influential friends.

'But for a few days, Valerie, you must stay in retirement while suitable garments are made for you. All you need will take much longer, but by the end of the week you should be able to appear presentable. I have sent word for Madame Elsa to come here at ten o'clock

25

tomorrow and start by taking your measurements. She will list the garments you need urgently. A very exclusive, and expensive, dressmaker, but I know I can rely on her judgement.'

'It is very kind of you, Aunt, but I have no money to pay for such luxuries. If I had not been so desperate I should not have hired myself out as a governess.'

'Your grandfather urged me to spare no expense when I left for England. He is prepared to settle all the bills.'

This proof of generosity from the old Count amazed Valerie. Did he, when he learnt of her existence, regret the cruel way he had treated his younger daughter and the non-aristocratic Englishman she was determined to marry?

When we do meet I must put aside thoughts of the humiliation Papa underwent. Papa and Mama would have wished me to do that, now Grandfather is being so good to me. I hope I can love him. I hope he is very different from Aunt Irma and Hugo. Does he realise how insincere they are? Anyway he refuses to believe Leonin is dead.

The mystery of Leonin baffled Valerie. She had been told that he paid a visit to relations in Russia and vanished on the return journey which was two years ago. Yet, according to Hugo, that disappearance was arranged by Aunt Irma through her powerful friend Prince

Metternich. He had been convicted of treason and sent to far-distant Siberia, a place that Valerie knew was where Russia kept its convicts. And Aunt Irma had done this to get Karpathy to herself and Hugo as soon as the old Count died.

When I reach Karpathy I can see it will be my duty to undeceive Grandfather.

But there were three months to wait. Valerie's heart sank when her aunt announced the arrival of a letter from the Count forbidding the party to leave Vienna until spring.

'Just what I expected,' commented Hugo. 'Winter is no time for travelling to Hungary.'

'Why not?'

'My dear Cousin Valerie, there are those unpleasant elements of snow and ice, far more severe in Hungary than in England.'

'How far is Karpathy from Vienna?'

'A few hundred miles, and progress is anything but swift. Hungary is undeveloped, not like Austria, and we can only travel by railway part of the way. The Alfold plain has no proper roads and one has to take a circuitous route by carriage to reach its eastern end where Karpathy Castle lies. Naturally Grandfather does not expect us until March when spring will start.'

Valerie was deeply disappointed but had not time to give way to feelings of frustration. During the first week in Vienna hours went by as she stood to be measured, for fabrics to be draped round her form, and then fittings. She was bewildered at the variety of gowns for all occasions, and the expensive accessories accompanying them.

Those initial days were exhausting, but the early mornings were leisurely when she could lie in bed until nine o'clock and enjoy the coffee and rolls brought by a maid. Every time this occurred she recalled the trials of governess days when the aggravating Pearson children had to be dressed, coaxed to eat breakfast in a civilised manner and restrained from fighting with each other. Lessons never began without further scenes, usually of defiance.

Breakfast in fashionable Vienna seemed more akin to luncheon for it did not take place until midday. Hugo was always at hand, and as soon as Valerie had a suitable outfit he took her and his mother to a fashionable hotel where they met a number of acquaintances. Valerie was included in an invitation to a musical party to be held the following week. She could see her life would soon become one of constant gaiety, but with Hugo always at her side. However important his government post he was free by midday, ready after the so-called breakfast to take her riding in the Prater. When winter set in, he told her he should take her sledging or skating.

He made no secret of his matrimonial

intentions. Valerie started by trying to ignore them, then tried treating them as jokes.

'Why won't you take me seriously?' he protested. 'I mean every word I say.'

'Don't be silly!'

'I love you and I want to marry you.'

'Marry penniless me! Utter nonsense!'

'You surely don't think I attach importance to mere wealth.'

'Any suitors do. That is why I shall never get a husband, because I am penniless.'

'Dear, sweet Valerie, you yourself are worth more than a necklace of jewels. Money, dowry—oh, you can't imagine I am such a worldly creature to care about those things.'

It was all Valerie could do to restrain herself from saying Liar! But what was the use? She was forced to endure Hugo and his mother until spring came and they could go to Karpathy Castle. She had always cherished an imaginary picture of her grandfather as a terrifying tyrant, but with her hatred of the two relatives lying to her, she began to change her ideas of old Count Karpathy. He persisted in believing against all odds that Leonin was alive, which did not look as if he wanted Hugo to inherit.

I might find I had more in common with him than with Aunt Irma and Hugo, she told herself.

But Valerie soon discovered that Hugo had no affection for Count Karpathy, only spoke of

29

him as a tyrant. In one unguarded moment, he actually revealed that during visits to Karpathy, right from childhood, he was scorned by the master of the castle.

'If he wasn't ignoring me he made me feel less than the dust by speaking to me in an icy voice. Mother used to be furious, only she was scared of making a fuss. Even now that Grandfather knows I am favoured by Prince Metternich he keeps up a pretence of believing Leonin is alive. Leonin must be the heir, not me.'

For a moment Valerie had caught a glimpse of a different Hugo. As if aware of this he made every effort to retrieve his normal poise, and vented abuse upon the missing cousin whom the old count had indulged, and whom he had disliked.

Leonin fancied himself a scholar, declared Hugo with scorn, and quite out of keeping with Hungarian nobility who were first and foremost sportsmen. But instead of boar or bear hunting, Leonin wanted to study abroad. A compromise was effected in which he went to Vienna University. 'Mother said it would be a good thing to have him under her eye, but of course she did not reckon on him secretly mixing with a set of left-wing students, rebelling against authority.'

'What happened then?'

'Oh, this invitation came from his grand

relations in Russia. They were intimate with the Tsar, though I doubt very much if Leonin got on well with them. The visit ended amicably enough, but you have heard how he disappeared on the way home, and no enquiries have unearthed his fate. Robbed and killed by brigands, I expect.'

'Why is there this secret rebellion against authority? I am sure we don't have it in English universities.'

'England was never really affected by the French Revolution.'

'The French Revolution! That happened a very long time ago. It is more than thirty years since Napoleon was defeated at Waterloo by our Duke of Wellington.'

'Oh, how you English boast about the Duke of Wellington! There were other fine generals, including Austrian ones who took part in ending the tyranny of Bonaparte. And it was in Vienna that the peace terms were drawn up. Austria first again! And it was during the Congress of Vienna that Prince Metternich became acknowledged as the greatest statesman of the age.'

'Tell me more,' asked Valerie but Hugo showed one of his sudden changes of mood, telling her politics and freedom and the like were no matters for women to worry about.

'But I want to know. I am interested in Leonin's left-wing views, as you call them. Who were these students he favoured when he was at the university?'

'Scum of the earth! But Leonin was such an oddity himself. That is why Grandfather agreed with Mother that a short spell at the Court of Russia would be an excellent thing for him. Unfortunately he had this accident on the return journey and it must have proved fatal.'

'But you don't know for certain he is dead.'

'Two years and no news! It is impossible he should be alive.'

Yet you believe he may be, thought Valerie.

'I've told you before that pretty little head of yours shouldn't concern itself with serious matters of state. Just fix it on your love for me.'

'I have no intention of doing anything so silly,' returned Valerie. She then fired a barrage of questions at Hugo. He had a Hungarian mother like herself so he ought to be interested in the country, and he hoped to inherit estates there. Could he speak the Hungarian language?

'Magyar, because the Magyars are the chief race living in Hungary.'

'What others are there?'

'Croats, Wallachs—oh, never mind. Aristocratic Hungarians like the Karpathys speak German or French, unless addressing servants and peasants. That agitator Louis Kossuth wants Magyar to be used officially.'

'Louis Kossuth! Who is he?'

'A great figure among the fools who want

change. They will never achieve anything, and Kossuth will be lucky not to be put in prison again.'

'But what does he do?'

'Talks, and edits a revolutionary paper that ought not be allowed. We Hungarian aristocrats have no use for such scum. Remember, dearest Valerie, you will soon be my wife and later mistress of Karpathy.'

'I don't want that fate,' began Valerie, but was silenced by feeling herself seized by Hugo and passionate kisses on her mouth.

She tried to get a hand free to hit his face, but he was too strong, pinning her close to him as he continued his slobbery kisses. This was Valerie's first experience of physical contact with a man, but she knew what would probably happen as he became more and more excited. She was terrified. The ideal lover of her dreams would not behave like this. He was pushing her to the ground. In another minute he would have her lying flat with his body on top of hers. She tried to kick him. Then she managed to scream.

Thank God, someone had come into the room and was saying, 'What is happening between you two naughty children?'

Aunt Irma's voice was partly playful but partly angry. It caused Hugo to loosen his grip on Valerie and scramble to his feet, while she, once released, rolled along the floor before pulling herself up by a chair.

33

'He has behaved abominably,' she stammered.

'Really, Hugo, this is not the kind of behaviour to show to a young lady. You must have taken leave of your senses.'

'Valerie knows I want to marry her, but she laughs at me every time I speak seriously.'

'I've told you definitely I will not be your wife.'

But Hugo continued in an aggrieved tone.

'You laugh and ask me stupid questions about politics. It is very insulting when a man talks of love.' He addressed his mother. 'She is the type who maddens a man. Leads him on, then refuses her favours. Something came over me just now. Well, I only meant to kiss her, but she behaved like a wanton, urging me on.'

'How dare you tell such a lie?'

'Valerie, dear, go to your bedchamber while I scold Hugo. He has behaved very badly and I am extremely angry with him. No wonder you are upset. Go to bed, and dinner shall be sent up to you on a tray. I will come when I have given this foolish son a piece of my mind.'

Somehow Valerie did not believe these protestations of sympathy which were out of character with the aunt she knew. For some mysterious reason marriage with Hugo had been planned by Aunt Irma, and the latter was not a woman to let anything interfere with a plan like that. She might chide Hugo for wrong

34

tactics. In fact she probably would...

Walking slowly upstairs, Valerie was certain that her aunt was still determined on this marriage, ridiculous when neither prospective partner cared for the other. A different type of girl, one like that banished maid Kataya whom Valerie had only heard, not seen, she would suit Hugo better than herself. And again came the puzzle why Aunt Irma should want a poverty-stricken niece for Hugo's wife.

He would do as he was told. For all his assurance, Hugo was clearly afraid of his mother and dared not disobey her order to make himself attractive to the cousin who had unexpectedly entered his life. Today he had lost control of himself and gone too far. Memories of those horrible kisses made her shudder, something she would not do if given by a man she really loved, she said to herself. For Valerie had grown up with parents who were still lovers. Even an innocent daughter could perceive that, also that Mama never regretted her sacrifice of home and family to marry Papa. These were confirmed beliefs although she recognised that the few romances she read gave too rosy a picture of matrimony.

'Your father has made me supremely happy and I hope that you will have the same good fortune with the husband you take, but remember, Valerie, these stories of romance do not go further than the actual marriage. A life follows when the woman must make every effort to understand and support the man she has vowed to love.'

Papa was a true gentleman in spite of Count Karpathy scorning him for non-aristocratic blood in his veins. And being an aristocrat did not make Hugo chivalrous. He was no better than her late employer's husband who was always pinching her backside. Fortunately Mrs Pearson kept a sharp eye on governesses and maidservants.

I hope Aunt Irma is making Hugo see how despicable he was just now, but I doubt it. She will come later to make excuses for him because she is so keen I should marry him. And why?

Aunt Irma had indeed turned in fury on her son. Dolt, fool, and other abusive epithets were hurled at him.

'You told me to get on with things.'

'Not like that! You know you went much too far and without proper preliminary wooing. You know better than that with all your experience of women. I shall say you had too much to drink.'

'Being a drunkard won't recommend me to her.'

'Naturally I shall tell the girl it was an unusual lapse, for generally you are very abstemious.'

'Then why are you always nagging at me for drinking too heavily?'

'Because I know you do, but Valerie had better be kept in ignorance of your weakness.'

'I had not been drinking much, but somehow the look of that milk-and-water English miss made me want to see if I could rouse any fire in her. I am a man with normal male feelings, Mother. You are a fool if you expect me any different.'

'I am expecting you to watch your step with Valerie because she is so inexperienced.'

'What a delightful wife!' sneered Hugo sarcastically.

'Marriage with her will be very much to our advantage. You heard what Tamas Szerb said. Why are you going out tonight?'

'Because I need a little gaiety. Oh, don't fuss, Ma, I will make the precious Valerie my wife. I won't be hurried though.'

'I shall make it generally known she has no dowry, but that you are wild about her in spite of that, and it is an alliance the Count Karpathy favours.'

'Good line to take, Ma!'

'So I do not want her antagonised against you. Underneath that meekness I can see your Aunt Lilla's obstinacy. Again I urge you, Hugo, do be sensible. Once married you will be master and can do as you like.'

'Unlike my pa.' Seeing an angry glint in his mother's eye, Hugo asked, 'Has Tamas Szerb got new papers ready?'

'I told him to do so, but I have not had a letter back yet. Mail travels so slowly from Hungary to Vienna.'

Her son chuckled. 'You fooled the ignorant Valerie when you led her to believe a reply had come from the imaginary letter you wrote to Grandfather. Was the correspondence achieved in one day, or two? Fortunately she did not notice the absurdity.'

'Go along to your restaurant and theatre,' said Aunt Irma irritably. 'I shall have a quiet meal by myself, then write a report for the Prince. He has heard Baroness Vangu is friendly with Kossuth supporters and suspects she is toying with that left-wing nonsense. At breakfast this morning she was defending Kossuth.'

'What would Prince Metternich do without a lady spy like you?'

'Don't use such a horrible word! I am no spy.'

'No, you just listen here and there, passing on tit-bits to the old Prince, and getting nice little cash rewards for your pains.'

The remark was ignored.

'I am going to soothe that child, though I really do not know how I am going to justify your behaviour in treating her as if she were a maidservant. Mind you control yourself in future.'

Irma von Moricz was very nervous as she

approached her niece's bedchamber. She would have liked to order Valerie to enter upon an instant engagement with Hugo, and marriage arrangements put in train immediately, but the girl would rebel, make scenes, and there was the faint possibility rumours might eventually reach Karpathy. She wanted the affair to appear perfectly natural in Viennese society. Lilla's story, though suppressed for years, was now being spread about, with the addition that old Count Karpathy wanted a match between Hugo and Lilla's daughter, and Hugo had fallen in love with his cousin at first sight. If only Hugo would act sensibly! He could have no rivals. The fact that this half-English, half-Magyar relative was dowerless would discourage the general mob of fortune-hunters in Vienna. Aunt Irma had thought out everything very carefully. As a last resort she could force Valerie to marry Hugo in secret, but she preferred to make the affair public with the bride willing. Tamas Szerb, her father's Administrator—title for a mixture of attorney and steward at Karpathy—it was his idea to present Count Karpathy with the married couple. The line of descent must be secured, and with Leonin dead, or imprisoned in Siberia for life, the old man would be compelled to name his heir.

Aunt Irma sailed into Valerie's room after giving orders to a footman to send along Magda, her personal maid.

She began, 'I am so very, very sorry about Hugo's naughty behaviour. You see, men, even the nicest men can behave unrestrainedly when they have had a little too much to drink.'

Magda came in at this point and was given orders for a light supper to be prepared and brought upstairs. When she had gone, Aunt Irma proceeded to excuse Hugo, assuring Valerie he never did drink to excess as a rule but he had been with an important visitor to Vienna. Prince Metternich left this gentleman in Hugo's care for breakfast, that turned out to be a meal where wine flowed at the guest's request, and though Hugo drank as little as possible it was more than he generally imbibed. He had rushed home thinking he would be late for dinner, but of course was not, and when he met Valerie he lost his head.

'You see the dear boy is so infatuated with you,' cooed Aunt Irma.

Valerie could hardly say she did not believe a word of it.

Aunt Irma warmed to the theme. She expounded it again and again. Valerie was the very daughter-in-law she had dreamt of.

'I cannot marry a man I do not love.'

'You will love Hugo as you get to know him better. Put down the tray Magda.'

Magda obeyed but did not hurry out of the bedchamber. Ignoring the maid, Aunt Irma said, 'Now do forgive the poor boy and think

40

kindly of him, my dear. He is very distressed, you know.'

'I will try to forget the whole incident,' said Valerie. 'But please will you and he stop talking about marriage. I hardly know him.'

'You are so different from your impulsive mother,' gushed Aunt Irma, kissing her niece. Valerie felt it was a traitor's kiss, and received it coldly.

'Have your supper, darling, and then you will feel better. See if Fraulein has everything she wants, Magda. I have important letters to write. Goodnight, my dear niece.'

The door closed behind Aunt Irma, and Valerie found herself looking into the deep-set dark eyes of the middle-aged maid who had been engaged because of her plain looks.

'You will feel better when you have had your supper, Fraulein,' came the maid's voice interrupting her.

Magda had seemed a colourless creature, not responsive to the kindly way Valerie always addressed her. As her services as abigail were almost exclusively devoted to Frau von Moricz, Valerie had little to do with her, and inwardly dismissed her as 'poker-faced'. Now she was surprised to see the earnest, sympathetic look in the woman's eyes.

It was more amazing when she spoke.

'Do not let the mistress or her son frighten you, Fraulein Valerie. If a marriage is being forced on you and you do not want that marriage, let me know. I have friends in Vienna with whom you could take refuge.'

'But I have no money.'

'That would not matter, I myself have never been to Hungary but they could get you there. Perhaps if you saw the old Count Karpathy personally, he might not insist you married Herr Hugo against your will.'

CHAPTER THREE

The very idea of being forced to marry against her will was a terrible possibility. No, it could not happen.

Aloud she asked Magda, 'Surely my aunt could not compel me to be Hugo's wife when I do not love him.'

'Frau von Moricz is a very definite person. When she has set her mind on something she is not easily turned aside.'

'Have you known her long?'

'No, Fraulein, but I heard about her before I took service here.'

'What made you become her abigail?'

'She engaged me through an agency. I happened to be available, and she was in a hurry to have someone before she set out for England to fetch you. She had dismissed my 'predecessor rather suddenly.'

'Yes, a girl called Kataya, whom she sent back to Hesse because my Cousin Hugo was carrying on a flirtation with her.'

'So you know about that, Fraulein.'

Unexpectedly they both laughed. It seemed strange to Valerie that the grave Magda could laugh and how this altered her entire face, changing her from an automaton into a pleasant human being. Valerie felt as if everyone she encountered in Vienna was acting a part. Magda certainly had been.

'You said just now that old Count Karpathy would not force me into a marriage I disliked.'

'That is a mere conjecture of mine, Fraulein. I have never seen the Count, only he appears to be on bad terms with Frau von Moricz so I imagine he will oppose plans she makes.'

'He was very unjust to my mother. She wanted to marry my father—an Englishman travelling in Hungary. And because Papa was not an aristocrat, Grandfather refused consent, and the only course open to Mama and Papa was elopement. You see, he was powerful enough, Mama said, to imprison her in the Castle and to have Papa turned out of Hungary.'

'But they succeeded in eloping?'

'They fled before Grandfather got wind of their intention, and after that, being Mrs. Gilliott, she was disowned. She never tried to

43

establish communication with him, so he had no idea I existed until I wrote to him after Papa and Mama were dead. I wrote to Karpathy Castle asking my grandfather to loan me money for me to take some other kind of training. He sent Aunt Irma to fetch me to Hungary.'

'Was his letter kind? Your parents' elopement was not your fault.'

'He has not written directly to me. Everything has been done through Aunt Irma, even the letter arriving here to say we are to delay our visit to Hungary until spring.'

Magda spoke decisively.

'No letter with the Count's seal has arrived here for Frau von Moricz.'

'But my aunt said one had.'

Magda made no reply. There was a lie here and Valerie believed the onus rested with Aunt Irma. She did not like her present position and it was a relief to discover Magda had friends with whom she could hide if Hugo tried to bully her into marriage. Perhaps those friends could assist her to earn a living, never mind if the job were a humble one. Not governessing, but she would be willing to work in a menial capacity, even that of housemaid.

'I have no money,' she told Magda.

'But you wish to reach your grandfather in Hungary, and without the von Moricz mother and son. Am I not correct in thinking thus? I can arrange that without you having to worry about money.'

'It is very good of you, Magda. Of course I do not know if my grandfather will prove sympathetic. He too may want me to marry Hugo. I just cannot understand why I am selected as his bride when I have no money, for my papa died in debt and I have nothing.'

'Your grandfather, I have heard, does not like Hugo, nor, I think, Frau von Moricz. He may take a fancy to you and wish to make up for the way he treated your mother.'

'I hope so,' said Valerie, though her tone of voice was anything but hopeful.

'Don't worry, you can count on my help in freeing yourself from the clutches of your cousin.'

Magda was about to leave the room when, seized by curiosity, Valerie stopped her.

'What is your nationality, Magda?'

'It was German, but my husband's was Hungarian, only he changed it to Austrian, and mine with his. He thought it safer for our son to be Austrian.'

'Does your son live in Vienna? How old is he?'

'Nearly thirty, Fraulein.'

'And what is his occupation?'

'He is a journalist, Fraulein.'

'You mean he writes for newspapers?'

Magda nodded, and as if unwilling to answer further questions she picked up the now empty

45

supper tray and left the bedchamber, uttering a polite wish that Fraulein would sleep well.

Valerie was to attend her first important social event the following evening. It was a musical party where celebrated artistes were engaged to perform. There was nothing frivolous about the affair. Guests were limited, among them being the Prince Metternich and his wife, while the hosts were among the Viennese élite.

Hugo had certainly modified his behaviour and was doing his utmost to atone for the previous lapse. He followed Valerie like a faithful dog, but a well-trained, submissive one, and though her dread of him began to fade she found him irritating. However, she was glad he had ceased to make jocular remarks, dropped his possessive attitude, and left it to his mother to introduce her to other guests.

When he did speak he merely supplemented very quietly any salient facts—usually of rank—omitted by Aunt Irma. Valerie realised her aunt was an important society figure and thought this entirely due to Frau von Moricz having originally been a Karpathy. Then she gathered from one lady's remark, 'Your aunt is so favoured by Prince Metternich,' that the connection with the all-powerful statesman counted for a great deal.

What did it involve? Valerie could not forget the mysterious disappearance of her unknown cousin Leonin and how she had overheard it had been achieved by assistance from Metternich. It disturbed her too that that intrigue—well, to speak plainly, crime, had been carried out without her grandfather's knowledge. When she reached Karpathy Castle she should certainly tell him the truth.

It does not matter whether or not he likes me, I shall do that. Mama would have desired it. Leonin is the heir and Aunt Irma is ready to do anything to pave the way for Hugo to succeed Grandfather.

The orchestra players sat with their instruments waiting for the arrival of Prince and Princess Metternich, since their performance would not begin until the illustrious guests were present. Valerie thought such lateness very rude. She was annoyed too by the way Aunt Irma had introduced her to a Countess Doeppel.

'The daughter of my younger sister whom our father, the present Count Karpathy, banished from home when she married below her rank. In fact, Lilla actually eloped with this Englishman. Both are dead now, so dear Valerie is under my charge until I take her to Karpathy Castle in the spring. My father wishes her to make her debut in Viennese society before she settles down to marriage. Oh, in this case it will be a marriage of which he approves. Valerie is too sensible to make a foolish misalliance like her mother.'

This made Valerie seethe with anger, especially as Aunt Irma coyly indicated Hugo who was standing just behind. It was a relief to recall Magda's promise of help.

At last Prince and Princess Metternich appeared and were greeted with great respect by the host and hostess giving the party. Aunt Irma was also beckoned forward. She sat by the statesman. His wife, a haughty-looking woman, had moved to a seat apart.

'She always does that,' whispered a lady to Valerie.

Hugo took up his position, standing behind Valerie until a footman brought him a chair and placed it next to her. After all this rearranging, the conductor took his place and the music began.

Valerie had been taught to appreciate good music, and now she listened, lost to her present surroundings and problems until the players finished. Then Hugo said his mother had told him he was to take her to Prince Metternich.

'Mother will present you,' he said, and with a flash of his former impudent manner he added, 'For heavens sake make a good impression on the old boy. She gets no end of favours from him, and I have my present job through her influence in that quarter.'

'Surely you could have a job without having to crawl to Metternich,' retorted Valerie.

'Especially as you don't need to earn your living. In fact, I thought Grandfather did not want any Karpathy to work, and you are his heir, unless the lost Leonin reappears.'

'Stop talking such rubbish!'

For a moment Hugo forgot his polite pose and sounded like the bully Valerie was sure he could be.

The next minute she found herself regarding the famous Austrian statesman whom she admitted must have been remarkably handsome in his youth. Even now, he retained a slim, graceful figure, deep-set alluring blue eyes, and well-moulded nose. He did not look over seventy, as Valerie had been informed he was, and at eighteen she naturally judged that was too advanced an age to be virtual dictator of the Austrian Empire. Of course there was an emperor, but she already knew Ferdinand was considered so weak in intellect as to be incapable of reigning.

A deep curtsey which was rewarded by a dazzling smile, and Aunt Irma formally presented her niece.

'Very charming,' said Metternich. 'And I gather you have not been able to take your position in English society because of your parents' deaths. My commiseration! I have met your young Queen Victoria. How long has she been reigning?'

'Ten years,' replied Valerie.

'How do you like Vienna?'

'Very much, Your Highness.'

Was that how one addressed him?

'She has not had the opportunity to know it properly yet,' interposed Aunt Irma. 'But Hugo intends to make up for such deficiency.'

She has told him that she wants Hugo and me to marry, was Valerie's impression.

To change the subject she announced how anxious she was to see Hungary, and that Count Karpathy was expecting the whole party in the spring.

Metternich gave an obvious yawn.

'I believe the journey to Karpathy Castle is long and tedious. Not that I have been so far east in Hungary. Pressburg, Buda, and Pest are the limits of my travel in that odious subject country.'

Aunt Irma cast a furious glance at her niece who had clearly said the wrong thing. She ordered Hugo to take Valerie for refreshments. 'The Prince desires other converse with me.'

'You made a blunder saying you wanted to see Hungary.'

'But why does Metternich hate the country?'

'Except for aristocratic families like the Karpathys, most Hungarians keep demanding liberty and independence. They want to be free from Austrian rule.'

'Why can't they?'

'Because Austria is the ruling power. You

50

should not have mentioned Hungary to Metternich. However, Mother is such a favourite she will soon restore him to good temper.'

'Does the Princess Metternich mind Aunt Irma being so friendly with the Prince?'

'Why should she? Females are Metternich's speciality. He has had three wives, four official mistresses, and many unofficial ones.'

Valerie was very shocked.

'Surely you aren't insinuating that Aunt Irma's friendship with him is anything unconventional?'

'What a child you are,' laughed Hugo. 'The Prince cultivates society hostesses like Mother so that he can obtain information on the tittle-tattle that goes on. Mother has a talent for relating stories that are both useful and amusing.'

'How extraordinary!'

For Valerie did not grasp that by tittle-tattle and amusing stories Hugo meant information on political matters, and he wisely refrained from opening her eyes to the personal espionage that made Metternich's sway over Austria so dangerous.

Musical parties and conversational gatherings were the most frequent type of entertainment, Valerie soon discovered. There was the occasional ball, and another new experience for her was a visit to theatre or opera. After the first evening when her enthusiasm for Hungary annoyed Prince Metternich, she managed to avoid making any other faux-pas.

During this time Hugo's behaviour was beyond reproach. She realised he drank too much, but he seemed to be keeping himself in check, probably due to scoldings from his mother.

She learnt from Magda that he had contrived to bring back the dismissed maid Kataya from Hesse, and installed her in an apartment rented for a mistress he no longer wanted.

'Do you think he is in love with the girl?' Valerie asked Magda.

'Love!' repeated Magda in disgust. 'From what I hear from other servants he always has a bit of skirt around for amusement.'

'Amusement, not marriage?'

'They are two separate things in Herr Hugo's mind. Like his mother, he is too set on his becoming the next Count Karpathy to consider marriage except with a member of the aristocracy like you, Fraulein.'

'The Karpathys despised my papa because he was not an aristocrat, so I am only part one and I have no money. I just fail to see how I qualify for Hugo's wife, apart from disliking him. Oh, Magda, I am relying on you to help me if there is a crisis, though I don't know why you should bother about me.'

'I will explain when the time comes. There

52

will be changes in Vienna because, sooner or later, Hungary will rise against its oppressors, particularly Metternich. But, Fraulein, if you accept my help you will become involved with freedom fighters.'

'I believe in freedom and justice, and I detest the way Aunt Irma and Hugo address servants, and their contempt for the farmers and peasants around Karpathy. They seemed to regard people who work on the estate as serfs. Do you think my grandfather is like that?'

'I do not know, Fraulein.'

But Magda's tone implied that he was likely to be imbued with the same beliefs. In that case, Valerie felt she should have little in common with him. Better to join these liberty loving friends of Magda, even if it meant hardship. Oh, why had dear Papa been so foolish about money! Mama believed financial matters were no concern of women, and she died without any idea of the weighty debts.

With just a small income, I could have lived modestly in England! I should not have written to Grandfather and thrown myself on his charity! Yet, what else could I have done?

In spite of a longing to go to Hungary and to see her mother's old home, Valerie was happy enough during the winter. By stifling the uneasiness regarding mistrust of her aunt and Hugo, and bolstered by the reliance she placed on Magda to provide an escape if matters became impossible, she admitted enjoyment of a social life hitherto unknown to her. Several young men paid her attention, but not seriously. Aunt Irma had made it clear to friends, who spread the news, that this niece had been left by improvident parents dependent on Count Karpathy's charity, while the Count was anxious for Hugo to marry Valerie.

'It will cement a family alliance,' she said vaguely. 'And Hugo is really wild about the girl.'

The great event of the New Year was a ball given by a wealthy diplomat for his daughter's coming-of-age birthday. The Baron Beckmann had not been long in Austria, but somehow had managed to establish himself and his family as newcomers to be flattered and generally toadied to. He spent money lavishly. His wife had become a favourite of the Princess Metternich. The question of an aristocratic genealogy was glossed over because of his diplomatic status, though Valerie overheard Hugo telling his mother the whole tribe of Beckmann seemed a 'jumped-up' lot and he was sure there was the taint of Jewish blood.

'The Metternichs accept them. This ball will be the event of the season, and naturally we shall go. Mind you behave yourself.'

Aunt Irma might have lectured her son further, but she saw Valerie listening and changed the subject to a discussion on dress.

The Beckmann ball had been planned with special regard to sensation. The first invitation issued specified fancy costume, but Princess Metternich immediately informed Baroness Beckmann this was a fashion out of favour at present in Vienna, so amended cards quickly followed the original. Aunt Irma had talked of Valerie being dressed as Queen Elizabeth of England, and Valerie, after seeing a picture of the Queen in elaborate attire, thought how uncomfortable dancing would be in such a costume. It was a relief to wear instead a pale pink velvet, designed in modern style, and trimmed with cream lace.

'I am disappointed because I was to have been Sir Walter Raleigh who placed his cloak on the muddy road for you to step on. Now, was it Sir Walter Raleigh, or somebody else?'

'Be sensible, Hugo,' said Aunt Irma, sharply tapping her son's hand with her fan.

By this time Valerie was well aware of her cousin's weakness for alcohol, and she considered he had been drinking too much when he joined them in the hall, ready to drive to the Beckmann mansion.

He was very talkative during the journey.

'Pity the Baron did not drop the notion of having a gipsy band and dancers as well as his fancy-dress scheme. Real gipsies are coming y'know, Valerie, taken from a camp outside Vienna, cleaned up, and dressed in respectable clothes the Baron has had made for 'em. They only come on to entertain us in the middle of the evening. He had to engage an ordinary orchestra for the proper dancing we enjoy.'

'I thought gipsies were vagabonds who moved about the countryside, telling fortunes at fairs.'

'Exactly so, my dear cousin. They never wash and their clothing is dirty and tattered. Oh, they are the scum of the earth! But Baron Beckmann heard of some crack-brained landowner in Transylvania who is supposed to have civilised a hundred or more of 'em, and now enjoys these creatures on his estate.'

'Absurd,' declared Aunt Irma. 'As if gipsies could be anything but filthy outcasts. Baron Beckmann is behaving as foolishly as the Count—oh, I forget his name—in Transylvania. I shall have my pomander ready to sniff while they are playing this gipsy music and dancing in a fashion we shall not appreciate. Still, Prince and Princess Metternich are countenancing our host's whim, so we cannot do otherwise.'

'Are these gipsies from Transylvania?'

'Good Lord, no! The Baron has hired them from a lot camping south of Vienna, and about to move into Italy for the winter. He has spent no end of money in cleaning them up and fitting them with so-called gipsy clothes—more like fancy dress which he wanted his guests to wear. Why must he do such nonsensical things!'

'But there will be a proper orchestra and proper dancing before supper,' said Aunt Irma. 'Now Valerie, you are to hand me your programme immediately you receive it. Hugo wants every other dance with you.'

'I should like every one.'

'Of course you would, but that would not be proper. Valerie's other partners I shall select for her.'

Valerie was in no doubt of the others being married men and much older than herself. While proprieties had to be observed, Aunt Irma was taking no risks lest her niece be squired by any male who could be remotely considered a rival.

The ball started with a round dance, was followed by a cotillion, then a waltz, and as a waltz partner Hugo was unbearable. He kept treading on Valerie's toes until she complained of thirst and insisted on them leaving the dance floor to drink glasses of almond tea, a beverage he accepted unwillingly. Aunt Irma smiled benignly as she whirled past, partnered by Prince Metternich.

'The old boy does find Mother useful,' remarked Hugo incautiously.

'Is Aunt Irma a spy for him?'

'What a word to use, my dear cousin. After all this is a police state so you ought to be careful what you say.'

The music ceased and other guests joined

them. Hugo encouraged company by loudly recommending the almond tea, but as soon as he could he slipped away to obtain stronger liquid. Valerie's next partner was a Captain Vogel, an elderly army officer said to be completely under his wife's domination.

Still horrified by Hugo's last remarks, she asked the Captain if the power wielded by Prince Metternich was bad for Austria, but he hotly denied such an idea.

'We are thankful for a strong chief minister, for our much respected Emperor is inclined to indulgence.'

'Indulgence to whom?'

'All the non-Austrian races who come under Austria's rule and keep making absurd claims for what some call self-government and others complete independence.'

'Is Hungary one of those?'

'Thanks to agitators like Louis Kossuth.'

'Tell me about him. I have heard the name before, but I know nothing about him.'

'Better for you not to know, my dear young lady.'

'But I am interested. I am half-Hungarian. Or should I say Magyar?'

'At present Kossuth is a Deputy in the Hungarian Diet that is held regularly at Pressburg, and trying to gain increasing power. He was elected last autumn. He has been stirring up trouble for years. Now he says he only wants Hungary's freedom from Austria, but for the Emperor to remain King of Hungary.'

Captain Vogel drew himself up sharply, saying again that politics were no subject for a young lady. It was with evident relief that he announced guests were taking seats set around the salon for the gipsy performance of music and dance.

The centre had been cleared for this. The regular hired orchestra players were leaving the salon, taking their instruments with them for safety, while at the same time casting contemptuous glances at the dozen gipsies who were being herded in by footmen.

Frau Vogel was sitting in the fourth chair from this entrance. Valerie was placed in the second by Captain Vogel, who thus sat between her and his wife, there being a vacant seat at the end.

'Herr Moricz will wish to sit by you, Fraulein.'

Hugo was still absent and Valerie fervently hoped he was not drinking hard to make up for the almond tea. He had grumbled so much about the squalor of gipsies that although these performers were presentable she felt certain he would dislike being so near them.

'You have a good view of the gipsy instruments,' Captain Vogel remarked. 'That broad stringed one is unusual. It is called a czimbalom and the strings are beaten with little hammers.'

Valerie looked at it, but her attention was claimed by the gipsies' costumes, more like fancy dress than their usual shabby, tattered old garments. These Baron Beckmann had obtained from a storehouse belonging to the Vienna theatre and opera companies. He had spared no expense to make this coming interlude a sensational feature of the ball.

The males wore long satin coats of either blue or crimson, trimmed with yellow braid and buttons, while their breeches and boots were dark brown. The two females had red kerchiefs on their heads, fancy blouses, and red petticoats bunching out, for each wore several, one on top of the other. Valerie was fascinated by their beads, bracelets, and anklets, which she realised must be cheap imitation jewellery, but the women flashed them as proudly as if wearing priceless gems.

Washing of visible parts of their bodies at least had been thorough, but no amount of water could remove the natural darkness of their skins, excepting that of the man sitting beside the czimbalom, and fingering his hammers as if impatient for playing to begin. He looked gaunt and as half-starved as the rest, but Valerie noticed how his weather-beaten face was lighter than those of his companions.

Hugo had not yet appeared, but to Valerie's embarrassment a young man seated himself in the vacant chair. She waited for Captain Vogel to state that seat was reserved, but the Captain was busy answering some question put by his wife and did not notice, and Valerie was diverted as she saw a delighted smile of recognition by the czimbalom player. Yes, the intruder was smiling back. These two must be mutual acquaintances. Her neighbour wrote a few words on a piece of paper, got up, handed it to the gipsy, then left the salon.

Valerie watched the recipient read the note then quickly put it somewhere on his person, for the Baron's steward and master of ceremonies announced that music, followed by gipsy dancing was about to start. It was strange music with wailing and ear-piercing notes varied by trillings. Valerie only listened mechanically at first because she was unable to take her eyes off the czimbalom player. He had actually read that note, but surely gipsies were too uneducated to have mastered the art of reading? Of course they read hands and cards when telling fortunes, but that was not proper reading. This man could not be a true gipsy, and she noted a certain air of pride that was alien to the others.

The music became quicker and dominated by a wild rhythm which had a curious effect on Valerie, rousing feelings she did not know she possessed. It was then the two female dancers came on the floor and their performance had a fire and abandonment that astonished her. She noticed Captain and Frau Vogel were looking shocked, and as her gaze wandered further there was the same look of disapproval on other faces. Baron Beckmann had misjudged the suitability of his entertainment for a conventional society audience.

There was no applause, only a deathly silence when the dancers retired and the music ceased. After a brief interval the gipsies were to continue, but the Baron summoned his steward, obviously giving orders that this was to be the end. As the servant walked to the gipsy leader Hugo appeared and began scolding Valerie for hiding herself away. He was drunk and spoke very loudly. His words were insulting too. Phrases like 'near those stinking low gipsies.'

Captain Vogel began to justify his choice of seat. Valerie turned away in disgust. She was sure the czimbalom player had heard the insulting remarks, for he was staring hard at Hugo. Then he picked up his instrument. Hugo had not noticed any of the individual players, who, with the two dancers, hurriedly shuffled out of the salon.

CHAPTER FOUR

Baron Beckmann's whim to have real gipsies performing at the ball was viewed with horror by his servants. They were only too ready to obey the order to get such dreadful vagabonds out of the house.

But first the gipsies had to exchange the hired garments for their old tattered rags, and to do this they were pushed down a flight of stone steps leading to a cellar which served as their dressing-room. At the rear came the czimbalom player, the steward holding a whip, and the man who had occupied the seat next to Valerie while writing his message.

'Who are you and what are you doing here?' demanded the steward.

'The Baron asked my society paper to send me here to make a report. Perhaps the order did not reach you, sir.'

'I remember now, but the Baron will not require any press notice about this affair after tonight's gipsy fiasco. You can leave the house straightaway.'

'Don't you consider, sir, that I ought to write a short paragraph and leave it with you to hand to the Baron? He can destroy it but I shall have accomplished the task for which I came.'

The steward agreed on condition nothing was

sent direct to the journal.

They had reached the bottom of the steps and, having settled the pressman's duties, he seemed about to order the czimbalom player to 'get a move on', but the pressman was handling the latter's instrument, and this particular gipsy seemed respectful and quiet, so the steward hurried on, leaving the two others to follow. Sounds of disagreement below, where the gipsies were quarrelling over their rags, made it necessary to assert his authority there.

However, he would not have acted thus if he had foreseen how the two young men would behave. The czimbalom was flung on a step while Kaspar began to guide his friend swiftly upwards, then along a corridor to a room at the end.

'I have been twice to this house so know my way around here. There is a side door close by, but there is something to do first.'

'But Kaspar, I cannot walk through the streets of Vienna like this. The garments will be so noticeable, soon traced to me and I shall be charged with theft before reaching the gipsy camp. I only joined the Zeugen-volk to carry out a secret revenge.'

'I live in Vienna—well, at present. It is my mother's house, but you can be assured of shelter and secrecy. As for getting there, this is the male guests' cloakroom, deserted at present. We'll both have protection against the cold

64

while you can choose a long cloak that will cover your fancy dress completely.'

This was soon done, and they emerged through the side door into a quiet street, turning quickly into a narrower one, then a maze of others. Soon they were in the older part of Vienna in a part where houses, though five or six stories high, were huddled together and obviously used as apartments with shops on the ground floor. Kaspar hurried his companion through a dark one that had ceased business for the night, produced a key, and carefully locked the door behind them.

'Wait until I get a few candles lit,' said Kaspar.

He was not long. The other ascended a narrow staircase which led directly into a comfortable square room with shuttered windows and four more doors opening from it.

'Kitchen and three bedrooms,' declared Kaspar. 'You never saw my old home, Leonin, but it was vastly superior to this. My father is dead and though he left Mother an ample jointure, she and I have special uses for our money. But we'll talk later. Come into my bedchamber and I'll find you some ordinary garments, though they will hang on you. Are you so thin through wandering with gipsies, or from your sojourn in Siberia?'

'How did you know I had been a convict in Siberia?'

'Later, later! Change, and I'll burn these hired theatrical costume objects. Then we will have supper. I can smell the stew Mother has prepared and left for me. After supper I'll tell you all I have been doing the last three years, and you can tell me your adventures.'

Leonin found himself in a small crowded bedchamber and watched his friend drag several articles of apparel from a cupboard.

'Must see to the stew. Bring the incriminating stuff with you and let's get rid of it in the stove.'

A huge porcelain stove heated the livingroom, as did smaller ones in other parts of the establishment. The hired so-called gipsy garments smoked badly at first, but this annoyance had no effect on the hungry Leonin. Kaspar had flung a cloth on the table and spread out cheap horn-handled cutlery. Then he filled a large bowl with stew and placed it before his guest who wasted no time in starting to eat. A bottle of wine was uncorked and Leonin drank from his glass with eager anticipation.

'The food of the poor Zeugen-volk was terrible, and in short supply.'

He used the Hungarian name for gipsies. Kaspar asked how his friend came to join the band.

'I wanted the opportunity to lurk round Vienna in disguise.'

'Surely you cannot be in danger now?'

'Danger?'

'As a convict who has escaped from a Siberian prison.'

'I was arrested in Russia on a false charge of treason and sent to Siberia, but one of my uncles, after difficulties and delays, saw the Tsar, and convinced him I was innocent. He obtained a pardon for me and I left Russia a free man. Uncle Michel discovered my accuser, though I already knew it was Aunt Irma's husband, acting on her instructions. It is on her I want to wreak vengeance. She is a despicable woman, a spy for Metternich, and I mean to make her pay for what she did to me. I decided first to learn her latest moves while keeping her unaware I was free. I have only just satisfied myself Aunt Irma and my cousin Hugo are in Vienna. What were you doing at that party, Kaspar?'

'Baron Beckmann wanted a report in a society journal, so the editor of the most fashionable one sent me, Kaspar Webber, to write it. As I glanced over the gipsies waiting to entertain the guests I saw you. Well, you got my brief note.'

'And overjoyed I was,' declared Leonin passing his bowl for more stew. 'I thought you were going to take up engineering work in Styria after your father died. I never expected to see you in Vienna. Of course I should have sought you in Leoben or one of the other Styrian iron towns, but I had no money, and the Zeugen-volk were granting me protection. They are on their way to warmer quarters until spring, and only waited near Vienna for this foolish entertainment. How shocked everyone looked!'

'The guests were indeed shocked. Baron Beckmann must be a fool. He wanted everyone to be in fancy-dress—a sort of masquerade without masks, but I understand he was told that would not do in the Vienna of today, where even Prince Metternich pretends to be proper and virtuous.'

'I definitely expected my aunt and cousin to be present, but not recognise me, and they did not. Hugo was too busy paying attention to a pretty girl. One of his many conquests!'

'That girl is also your cousin for I heard her addressed as Miss Gilliott, and my mother has talked a good deal about her. Oh, I have so much to tell you, Leonin, that I don't know where to start. Are you *au fait* with the present state of affairs in Hungary?'

But Leonin's thoughts were occupied with the information that he had a cousin whose name was Gilliott, and was apparently English.

'Gilliott was the name of an Englishman who eloped with my Aunt Lilla. An affair never to be mentioned since she disgraced the noble Karpathy family by such a low alliance, and one forbidden by my grandfather. As a child I learnt about the affair from my old nurse, but I was too young to remember Aunt Lilla properly.'

He had a dim vision of the aunt who played with him, kissed him a lot, and smelt of flowers. Once he pinched her arm playfully and she just smiled. So the girl he had seen close to the gipsy musicians must be her daughter.

Kaspar was explaining briefly the few facts he had learnt about Valerie from his mother, concluding with Frau von Moricz's plan of marriage with Hugo, and how Magda would help her to escape from it if necessary.

'She wants to go to Karpathy, but Mother will hide her here, and perhaps she will help with our underground work.'

'How does your mother come into this?'

'Mother, like me, is a secret agent for Lajos Kossuth.'

Leonin was immediately absorbed in the fate of this hero whom he and other university students had worshipped a few years ago.

'Tell me the latest about Kossuth. Remember I have been cut off from all news because the Zeugen-volk knew nothing of state affairs. Is he still leading the struggle for Hungary's independence?'

The subjection of Hungary to Austria was hateful to Leonin, Kaspar, and their friends, as well as to the majority of Magyar people.

Kossuth had founded a national league to become a centre of opposition to the Viennese government. He was a member of the Hungarian Diet, a local parliament whose powers were always being checked, and the rebellious Kossuth was imprisoned at one time. Only his extreme popularity induced Metternich to permit his release, then try to win him over. After all, Kossuth wished not to interfere with the Emperor, but to keep Ferdinand's function as King of Hungary separate from that of Austrian Emperor.

'I demand,' he had declared, 'that the free soil of Hungary should be inhabited by free men.'

Dangerous words, and in his younger days Metternich would have got rid of a man who uttered them. Now, unaware of the strong underground movement which was rapidly expanding, he allowed the Kossuth affair to drift. Instead he concentrated on reports brought by his spies—police agents whose work was confined to Austria, and the society gossip of women like Irma von Moricz. The Hungarian peasants, he assumed, were easily controlled by their noble masters. Metternich overlooked the fact that the majority of noblemen spent little time on their estates but enjoyed the gay society of the Austrian imperial court. Count Karpathy was an exception, but he was not a humane overlord, according to his grandson.

Leonin said, as the possibility suddenly struck him, 'I expect my grandfather is wondering where I have been these last two years, because I was arrested through being deliberately mistaken for someone else and given no chance to prove my real identity. Yes, I must send word of my being in Austria to him, though I have no intention of wasting years at Karpathy quarrelling with the old boy over his brutal injustices, which I shall sweep away when I become Count. I suppose he is still alive.'

'Oh, he is alive, and he refuses to believe you dead.'

'How have you got this information, Kaspar?'

'I'll explain in a minute, but first I am asking you to remain hidden in Vienna, or wherever we are sent. I am imploring you to join the organisation working to set Hungary free from Austria. An explosion will come soon—probably in the spring. We are just waiting and working.'

'For Kossuth?'

'Yes, and the ideals he stands for. That is why Mother gave up our home in Leoben, and we are putting up with this shabby place. We could not work from a large conspicuous mansion. You believe in our cause, don't you?'

'You convinced me when we were university students here,' said Leonin gravely. 'Not that I needed much conviction. You know how disgusted I was with the way my grandfather ruled Karpathy. To him and his kind, land and those who work on the land are meant to be exploited for the nobility's benefit, and once I realised this I vowed to behave differently. Yes, I'll remain here and help as long as I am needed. Karpathy Leonin does not break his word.'

He used the old Hungarian custom of putting surname before christian name.

'Thanks,' replied Kaspar. He poured out more wine for them to drink as a pledge.

'And now, how did you learn about my arrest in Russia?'

'My mother, I told you, belongs to the underground movement which is seeking liberation for Austria from Metternich, while we also want Hungary to have independence in most matters. That is Kossuth's dream. Well, Mother helps by having obtained a position of abigail under one of Metternich's noted spies, your aunt, Frau von Moricz. Mother overheard a conversation between that lady and Herr Hugo Moricz about you being a prisoner in Siberia. It was their doing, and they were proud of it.'

'A convict in Siberia! I was taken some thousand miles across eastern Russia until at last we reached a prison settlement in that bleak, lonely country, and there I should still be

72

if I had not had an influential relative. My cursed Aunt Irma and Hugo will naturally assume I shall never re-appear to claim my inheritance and denounce them.'

'But why did you join the Zeugen-volk? Have you no passport or other papers?'

'Indeed I have, and respectable clothes, but I left them with old Hans.'

'Hans who was your servant at the university?'

'He is still there, faithful and trustworthy. He asked no questions, but took my goods, informed me of the Zeugen-volk camp if I wanted to hide, and because I could play the czimbalom, I was accepted. I thought that disguised as one of them I could track down Aunt Irma and Hugo, but it was not easy because we were not allowed to enter the main streets of this city. I had not realised how impossible it would be to get near the aristocratic quarters, and this camp of Zeugen-volk was journeying south. I prepared to leave them when I heard of Baron Beckmann's show. And I was certain Hugo would be there. He must be in Vienna because of the government post he holds. My aunt's husband died after doing her dirty work in getting me sent to Siberia. My uncle told me that. As for Aunt Irma, she prefers living in Vienna and being useful to Metternich, while my grandfather hates her. I was sure she would be at this party, and I went with the intention of proclaiming publicly who I was and how she had treated me, but I saw that would be hopeless. Oh, I'll have my revenge!'

'Surely disgracing her in your grandfather's eyes would be more effective.'

'She and her son have never been favourites with him.'

'But Frau von Moricz is trying to make Count Karpathy accept your death and announce her as heiress to his estates.'

Leonin laughed.

'My mother found that out,' said Kaspar.

'Impossible! There is a distant male branch of the Karpathy family that Grandfather hates, but he would make the eldest his heir if he believed me dead. Yes, two years since he had news of me is a long time. I must write, but give no clue to my whereabouts. I have promised to help in Kossuth's cause, and I will. Now tell me more about the girl, Aunt Lilla's daughter. If she has any sense she won't marry Hugo Moricz.'

'She doesn't want to marry him, so Mother says.'

'Why is she in Vienna?'

'Her parents are dead and Count Karpathy sent Frau von Moricz to fetch her from England. Wait until Mother calls here. She'll give you details which, frankly, have not interested me.'

'When do you expect your mother?'

'That I never know. She slips along here at night when Frau von Moricz is asleep in bed, or out at a party. I may not see her again until she brings a report for our underground movement on something important she has heard.'

An entire week passed before Magda came again. Meanwhile Leonin had recovered his belongings from Hans, but found it policy, so as not to attract attention, to dress in less expensive garments that Kaspar obtained for him.

'You still look an aristocrat,' complained the latter. 'Keep indoors as much as possible.'

'This cloak you bought secondhand is surely shabby enough, and it covers me better than the one you took from Baron Beckmann's.'

'Yes, but you walk with a nobleman's air. Can't you stoop and shuffle? Then you would look more like an artisan.'

'I'll try,' said Leonin without enthusiasm.

However, there was no need for him to go out except occasionally at night when he accompanied Kaspar to meetings of the underground movement. Winter had set in and the darkness was an extra cover. Only once did he see the hero Kossuth and was impressed by the ardour of those assembled, also by the intensity of the leader's pale oval face, and still more by his fervent words. He was not merely a politician but the voice of an oppressed people, the Hungarians, though despite a general wish for their freedom Kossuth's first thought was for his country. Next day he was going to its ancient city of Pozsony, generally known by the Austrian name of Pressburg, where the Hungarian Diet met. Kossuth had been elected a member a few months previously, and was already trying to have its limited powers increased.

'We ought to go to Pozsony,' Kaspar told his friend. 'I must send word to Mother and then we will follow Kossuth. We shall be needed there or in Pest in the spring.'

Kaspar was expecting some outbreak of action then, and he frequently referred to it. Plans were vague, but there was to be a rising of some kind, and rights demanded from the Emperor Ferdinand. Leonin had given his word to help, putting aside all personal matters for the time being. Now he regretted this. He longed to return to Karpathy, show the old Count he was still alive, and proclaim Frau von Moricz's treachery. Although his ideas were opposed to those of his grandfather, and since boyhood he had defied the Count, yet he loved Karpathy, home of his forebears, and the great Alfold plain around the estate. Winter's heavy snow did not deter him from longing to attempt the journey.

But he could not attend to his own affairs while Kaspar and the underground movement claimed him.

I gave my word, he repeated regretfully to himself.

Revenge must wait. He did not even send word to his grandfather that he was alive and in Vienna. Time enough when he was free of obligations. Nothing could alter his legal right of inheritance, however much he displeased the Count.

Leonin was alone and cutting up vegetables and meat for the stewpot when he heard a key being inserted in the outer door. Leaving his domestic work he went to investigate and nearly collided with a small dark woman, whose quickness of movement was the first thing about her that struck him. Then he realised from the resemblance between her and his friend that she was Kaspar's mother. Kaspar had the same kindly but almost simian appearance.

'Good day, Frau Webber.'

'I have not met you before.'

'No, I am an old friend of Kaspar, but I have been in Russia for three years...'

'Heavens! Are you Leonin Karpathy?'

Magda seized both his hands.

'So you have actually escaped from a Siberian prison...'

'No, Frau Webber. I am not so clever as that. One of my mother's brothers secured my pardon.'

They sat down, both preparing the stew,

while Magda made Leonin describe his adventures in detail, and remarked with grim satisfaction that it would be a very unpleasant shock for Frau von Moricz.

'Yes,' said Leonin. 'I hear you are working as abigail for my abominable aunt. I am sure she never imagines I can reappear, but she shall have that shock eventually. I shall deal with her in my own time. First I have promised to help Kaspar in the struggle led by Kossuth, so my own affairs must wait until that is achieved.'

'Are you wise?' asked Magda.

'What do you mean?'

'Should not you visit your grandfather before you become otherwise involved? Your aunt is intriguing against you. That is why she had you put in that far-away prison. She wanted you out of the way so that she could become Count Karpathy's direct heir.'

'My Aunt Irma the heir! That is ridiculous.'

'It is how she and Herr Hugo talk.'

'But she can never claim any rights of inheritance. There are distant cousins who would see to that if I were dead.'

'I understood the daughter of an Hungarian nobleman could inherit, failing a male heir.'

'A proper daughter, and her offspring. Now this girl, what is her name?'

'Valerie Gilliott.'

'She is English, but her mother was a Karpathy, and Valerie was born in wedlock.

Well, wasn't she?'

'Yes, but Valerie's mother was younger than your father. Frau von Moricz must be a good deal older than either.'

'Older, but illegitimate. Didn't you realise she was my grandfather's bastard daughter?'

Leonin smiled sardonically as he saw the look of amazement on Magda Webber's face. Just then Kaspar joined them, having let himself in with his own key, and the situation had to be explained to him. But Kaspar was too absorbed by his own mission and in studying the latest report brought by Magda on her mistress's society spying, to give much attention to facts about Leonin's family. In fact he begrudged Leonin wasting time in replying to his mother's questions.

Count Karpathy, like other Hungarian nobles, exercised a *droit de seigneur* over servants or peasant women he fancied, but Adel Vavell, daughter of a minister of religion, aroused love as well as passion. Marriage was out of the question, and before the child was born the Count banished the minister and his pregnant daughter to Miskolcz. Years later the Count allowed the illegitimate Irma to live at Karpathy Castle. By this time he had married suitably, as was his duty. The bride was an Hungarian aristocrat, and the marriage was celebrated in grand style. It produced two children, Leonin's father Julius, and Valerie's mother Lilla.

'I was only a small boy and I can scarcely remember Aunt Lilla,' Leonin told Magda Webber. 'It was forbidden to mention her name.'

'Valerie says she is sure Count Karpathy was unaware of her existence, or her parents' death, until she wrote begging his assistance in training for other work. She hated being a governess.'

'She was surely lacking in pride to write so.'

'But she was desperate. When you are orphaned and penniless, life is very hard. Oh, Valerie hated writing to the Count, but he was unexpectedly kind and sent Frau von Moricz to bring her to Hungary.'

'Then why is she still in Vienna?'

'It is said to be on Count Karpathy's orders. Certainly the rest of the journey can be unpleasant in winter.'

'Snow is unimportant,' declared Leonin. He sounded as if he thought the excuse a feeble one.

'Frau von Moricz talks about herself in Vienna as heir to the Karpathy estates, which she will immediately pass to Herr Hugo. She insists you must be dead as nothing has been heard of you for so long.'

'But she is my grandfather's bastard and he will never permit her to inherit. It would be illegal. And though her mother was supposed to have captured his heart more than others he

80

summoned to his bed, he soon forgot her. Then the old Administrator died, and the new one, Tamas Szerb, is a nephew of the old minister Vavell, I think. Anyway, when Aunt Irma was about thirteen, he prevailed upon Grandfather to take her from the care of her mother in Miskolcz and let her live at Karpathy as a sort of superior maid and seamstress, but Grandfather apparently treated her like dirt. Somehow she went to Austria and there met this German of good family who wanted to marry her. Grandfather approved, so she and her husband, and Hugo when born, came to the Castle on occasional visits.'

'You must have been quite small then?'

'I wasn't born until Hugo was four. Neither he nor Aunt Irma have the slightest claim to Karpathy. I am the legitimate heir.'

As if it had suddenly occurred to him, he added, 'If I had died in Russia, then the heir would have been Aunt Lilla's daughter.'

'Valerie! So that is why your aunt wants to marry her to Hugo.'

'The girl will be a fool if she consents. Certainly, with me out of the way and this Valerie Hugo's wife, he could secure the estate through her. Any husband owns property inherited by his female partner. What a cunning alliance!'

'Fraulein Valerie says she will not wed Herr Hugo,' declared Magda. Ignoring Kaspar's

81

impatience, she expressed the wish that Leonin could meet Valerie, although she was forced to acknowledge this would be difficult to arrange.

'It is awkward for me often to come here. I have to choose a time when I am certain Frau von Moricz will not be demanding my attendance. As one would expect with any young society girl, Valerie only goes out accompanied by her aunt or cousin. A mere abigail like me is never sent to escort her. That we are on friendly terms is unknown to Frau von Moricz.'

'Friendly terms?'

'I have promised Fraulein Valerie I will help to hide her if there is any attempt to coerce her into being betrothed to Herr Hugo. I can tell her now that you are alive, and what you have said about her aunt being illegitimate, and that I will arrange a meeting between you two when it is possible.'

'No,' interposed Kaspar. 'None of today's talk should be repeated to Fraulein Valerie. Mother had better keep everything secret at present. Don't you agree, Leonin?'

Unfortunately he did, and Magda did not feel disposed to argue with her son. All the same, she wished she could bring the two cousins together. Valerie ought to know Leonin was alive, also the full extent of the intrigue regarding marriage between her and Hugo.

CHAPTER FIVE

Secrecy of which she did not approve weighed heavily on Magda and caused her to avoid contact with Valerie. This was easy since Irma Moricz had no intention of sharing the abigail's services with her niece. By now she had ceased to send Magda to Valerie's bedchamber just before a large function so as to put finishing touches to the girl's toilette. That had been a great favour.

Valerie sensed a change in Magda's manner in Aunt Irma's presence, but put this down to increased caution in keeping their 'understanding' secret. It was not in her nature to doubt Magda's promise to hide her with friends if Aunt Irma insisted on announcing a definite betrothal to Hugo. During the two months following Christmas her aunt made no frightening remarks. She seemed content for Valerie to dance half the evening with Hugo at balls, and to accept his escort at theatres and outdoor activities. The last-named were often skating parties where there was plenty of other company, as at an evening festivity.

Yet Valerie was uneasy. Magda once told her that the dismissed German maid, Kataya, had not been banished to Hesse as Irma von Moricz intended and that she was now in Vienna as

Hugo's mistress.

Valerie wished he would marry the girl, but she knew circumstances of birth prevented that, even if Hugo cared sufficiently. From his outspoken declarations she was repeatedly informed he adored her, penniless Valerie Gilliott, and took it for granted she would eventually become his wife. According to Aunt Irma, 'the dear boy' was hardly touching strong drink, and openly gave her niece credit for the reformation.

Valerie knew there was no such reformation. She knew too that her aunt was ignorant of Kataya's presence in Vienna.

February was at its end when a general atmosphere of alarm pervaded Viennese society. Politics meant nothing to Valerie, but when she heard everybody talking about another revolution in France, forcing King Louis Philippe to abdicate, she realised serious events were happening abroad. She had been taught about the French Revolution of 1789, with the subsequent executions of King Louis XVI and his consort. Was a similar tragedy to happen again?

Valerie heard of this new rising in France while she was attending a ball at the Metternich Palace. It so horrified her that she could think of nothing else, and she was very surprised the rest of the company did not appear particularly affected, taking it for granted that what happened in France would have no influence on an empire under the strong arm of Prince Metternich.

There was much whispering and Valerie became conscious of glances directed at herself. Why should she be the subject of any general chit-chat? Then she realised why. There was an interval in the dancing. She found Hugo standing beside her, seizing her arm and saying Prince Metternich was asking for them both.

'Why?'

'He agrees with Mother that it is time matters were settled.'

'What matters?'

He made no attempt to answer, but led her to the throne-like armchair where, like a monarch, sat Metternich with the Princess Metternich on his left and Aunt Irma standing just behind the two. Hugo bowed and Valerie curtsied. There was a smug look on his face that filled her with apprehension, and this was justified when Metternich took her hand, placed it in Hugo's, and announced that Frau von Moricz had granted him the privilege of publicly declaring the betrothal of Herr von Moricz to Miss Gilliott, English cousin of that esteemed gentleman.

Like an automaton, Valerie found herself acquiescing in this maddening state of things. But only for this evening, she told herself. A toast was drunk. Then the orchestra began to play again and, ordered by Metternich, she and Hugo led off the first dance, while all the time she kept repeating to herself that she would not allow this farce to continue once the party was over. She could do nothing until they left the Metternich Palace.

Even then came delay. A friend of Hugo, and it was obvious both had been celebrating the betrothal, came part of the way, leaving the von Moricz carriage at the friend's house. Hugo said he would walk the remaining short distance, but his disapproving mother insisted the carriage would return to collect him.

At last came the opportunity for Valerie to face her aunt. She tried to draw her from hall to withdrawing-room, but Irma seemed indifferent to what the footman on duty might hear.

She turned on Valerie.

'It is useless for you to protest. Hugo wishes to make you his wife, as you must have realised these weeks by his attentiveness. It is exactly what your mother would have wished.'

'How can you say that? Before my mother died you had not seen her for at least eighteen years.'

Irma von Moricz continued as if Valerie had not spoken.

'You need the protection of a husband since you are without parents or money. Look at the position I found you in—a girl with Karpathy blood in her veins teaching bourgeois children!

That was the fate I rescued you from.'

'You came to London to take me to Hungary on the order of my grandfather, and I do not understand why there had to be months of delay before going to his castle.'

Again she was ignored.

'It is also according to the orders of Count Karpathy that you are to marry Hugo.'

'I don't believe that,' retorted Valerie. 'I shan't believe it until I hear it from my grandfather's own lips, so the sooner we set out for Hungary and I see him in person the better. I know he is prepared to forgive my mother and to receive her child. Otherwise he would not have sent you to England to fetch me. Surely he has no reason for delaying our meeting.'

Irma gave a contemptuous laugh.

'That is all you know. I actually received a letter from my father the Count today approving a marriage between you and my son. In fact he directs that you two are to wed before we all go to Karpathy.'

'I don't believe you. Before making such a proposal he must surely want to see me in person.'

'It is no proposal but a command. He hates the very name of your father, and although he is prepared to accept you as Lilla's daughter and forget her wicked defiance and misalliance, yet he has no intention of receiving you at Karpathy Castle until you have legally rid yourself of the surname Gilliott. You will go there as a Karpathy, or not at all.'

'Then I shall not go there at all,' declared Valerie in fury.

'Grand words, my dear niece, and where do you propose to stay in Vienna? You have no money, either for lodgings or for your return to England. I don't see you getting a governess post here. Do not talk in a way that lays you open to ridicule.'

Valerie pretended to be awed by her aunt's words, but inwardly she was determined to ask for the help promised by Magda and escape into hiding with the latter's friends, no matter what politics they held. Anything was better than remaining a pawn in the strange game her aunt was playing. Her grandfather's behaviour was a mystery to her. As for marrying the alcoholic Hugo, who was really absorbed in the maid his mother had dismissed—never, never!

She vaguely heard her aunt saying she should see Count Karpathy's letter in the morning, and wondered cynically if it existed or was to be written by her aunt that very night. She hardly heard Irma's scornful rebuke when she said the Count ought to have ascertained her feelings.

'He should have written direct to me, and asked if I were in love with Hugo, which I am not.'

'You expect the Count to concern himself with that nauseating emotion called love. All he wants is absolute obedience to his wishes, and those wishes include a marriage of which he approves. You have some ridiculous notions in that stupid head of yours, Valerie, notions I advise you to discard at once. Anyway, I have no intention of listening to your chatter. And don't wait up for Hugo because he won't want his happy evening spoilt. The sooner you realise you are being asked to become wife to a man in a million, the better.'

'A man in a million indeed!'

But Irma had swept out of the withdrawing-room. Valerie sat down on a small chair with her head in her hands. Whether her grandfather's views were correct or not, and certainly Aunt Irma had given varying versions of them, it was time to take advantage of Magda's offer of help. She must escape and remain hidden. No matter what kind of people, law-abiding or revolutionaries... Valerie felt she could not endure the von Moricz household another day. It was worse than being a governess in England. Mrs Pearson had been an unkind, bullying employer, but Aunt Irma and Hugo were positively evil.

The next step was to find Magda, get her alone, and invoke the aid that had been offered. However Valerie had no idea where Magda slept, so she must contact her in Aunt Irma's bedchamber, provoke another row with her aunt, and from this Magda would realise help was needed. Guessing she would be preparing her mistress for bed, Valerie walked into the grand bedchamber on the first floor without knocking. Aunt Irma was standing by her toilette table as Magda unfastened the tiny hooks on her evening gown.

'How dare you intrude upon my privacy? Go away immediately. I have told you I have nothing more to say to you.'

'But I have to you, Aunt Irma. Although you persuaded Prince Metternich to make a public announcement of betrothal between Hugo and me this evening, this was without my permission. I could not make a scene in front of the Prince and his guests, but I am telling you now that nothing will induce me to continue with this so-called betrothal. I will not marry your son.'

'You will marry Hugo. Go to your bedchamber at once. If there is any more nonsense I shall put you under lock and key.'

In menacing fashion Irma picked up a hairbrush from the toilette table, advanced towards Valerie, and would have struck her but Valerie quickly dodged the blow. She managed to cast an appealing look at Magda, then left the room. Magda would get the message. She would understand.

Once in the privacy of her own bedchamber, a floor higher, Valerie lit the candles, then locked the door against unwanted intrusion although she did not think Aunt Irma would seek her out again that night. She changed into a day gown and short boots, put out a warm cloak, and began to fill a valise with what she considered absolute necessities.

There was a gentle knock at the door, repeated when no answer came, and after that a low call of 'Fraulein Valerie.'

Hearing Magda's voice Valerie rushed to unlock the door. The sight of her dressed in a plain day gown won immediate approval.

'Your aunt has sent me to lock you in and take the key to her, so I am thankful you are ready to leave. Delay might make her suspicious.'

'She means to make me a prisoner. How dare she!'

'You want me to take you to—safety, don't you, Fraulein?'

'I have been relying on you to keep your promise, Magda, for I am determined to get away from Hugo. Prince Metternich publicly announced our betrothal tonight, and you heard the second row I had with my aunt over the affair. Please take me to your friends.'

Magda pushed down the lid of Valerie's valise, put the cloak round the girl's shoulders, and ushered her out of the room, locking the door as she did so.

'Once I have handed Frau Moricz the key, she will assume you have gone to bed. I shall

91

have to disrobe her, but once she has dismissed me I can get away. Hide in this cupboard until I come.'

The cupboard was some distance along the landing, and here Valerie hid, but found the wait long and unnerving. At last Magda came back and together they descended three back staircases, none of which Valerie had used before, and was surprised at their narrowness and lack of carpeting. She was sure the valise was too heavy for Magda to carry, but help was impossible until they could walk two abreast.

Close to the end of the last flight was a back door, bolted and locked, but as Magda flashed the small lantern she was carrying on it, Valerie saw the key had not been removed. Magda put down the valise, which Valerie tried to lift but found it very heavy. She should not have packed extra footgear she told herself. Magda slid back the bolts noiselessly, then turned the key, and Valerie saw there was a small patch of ground containing privies and a path that led to another gate, bolted and locked like the other but again with the key left.

'We'll leave your case,' said Magda. She opened the door and, after Valerie had gone through, pulled it shut, but being unbolted and unlocked it would be simple for an outsider to push it ajar.

'I shall come back with my son,' Magda explained. 'I want to remain with your aunt for

I have work to do in watching her. That is why I must be careful she does not suspect I have had anything to do with your escape.'

'But my valise?'

'Kaspar, my son, will return with me and pick it up. Then I go inside and bolt and lock both doors. You see, Fraulein, I am really a spy like your aunt, only I work for freedom and liberty, she for tyranny as represented by Prince Metternich.'

'I am on the side of freedom,' declared Valerie, as they walked along.

'What would your grandfather the Count say if he heard you make such a declaration?'

'My grandfather is a mystery to me. I cannot understand his attitude and how he seems to change orders. Certainly when I first appealed to him for help, he sent Aunt Irma to fetch me from England, but I understood we were going immediately to Karpathy Castle, yet I am still in Vienna. Now she says he will not receive me until I am Hugo's wife.'

'It is always what Frau von Moricz says, isn't it, Fraulein? Do not believe anything until you hear it from your grandfather's own lips.'

'But I am not likely to meet him now I have run away from Aunt Irma.'

'You may,' said Magda mysteriously. She wanted to tell the girl about Leonin's return, how he said their aunt was illegitimate, and that the reason for making Valerie marry Hugo was because Valerie was the heir until Leonin reappeared, but there was no time for such explanations during the hurried walk to Magda's house.

Valerie began speculating what her aunt would say when she found Hugo's proclaimed betrothed was missing.

'I hope she does not suspect you, Magda.'

'No, why should she? She has no idea of the times I have slipped out when she was asleep or at a big society function. But I had to see Kaspar. She does not know I have a son and a home here in Vienna.'

Valerie had no idea what to expect from Magda's home, so she was surprised to find it consisted of rooms over a shop. The shop, now dark and empty, did little genuine trade in the brassware and china it stocked. Magda explained it was a screen for members of the underground movement, and here Kaspar received communications.

Curiosity to see Kaspar mounted in Valerie as she followed her hostess up the stairs and watched Magda unlock yet another door. There was an austerity, one could hardly term it poverty, about the hall-cum-living-room, but it was warm and comfortable, and the furniture was of good quality.

'I must wake Kaspar and urge him to dress quickly. We want your case, while I cannot delay my return. Not that Frau von Moricz is likely to wake and ring for me tonight, but I want to shut the doors I left unlocked and bolted. You wait here, Fraulein, until Kaspar comes back.'

Magda went to her son's bedchamber and Valerie wondered how he was receiving the explanation of her sudden appearance. Yes, Magda had said there was perfect amity between the two, so he could not object to a guest, especially one willing to work for the downfall of a tyrant like Metternich. Meanwhile Valerie went to a large mahogany bookcase standing against a wall and began to scan the book titles it contained. She had not finished when the two Webbers appeared, and she had the opportunity to see Kaspar.

He was very like his mother she decided, and had the same jerky quickness of movement. At the moment his dark eyes were sleepy and he had obvious difficulty in suppressing a yawn, but his greeting was polite enough. He shared Magda's feeling that haste was important. Valerie noticed he was dressed for going out, and the two set off immediately.

All Magda said was, 'Kaspar will arrange about your sleeping accommodation when he returns, and explain everything else. Now Fraulein dear, you will have to remain indoors for the present in case anyone who knows your aunt sees you. It would be fatal if she found out where you were hiding. However Kaspar

95

expects to go soon to Pressburg...'

'Pozsony, Mother,' corrected Kaspar, using the old Hungarian name. 'I won't be long, Fraulein.'

Left alone Valerie sat down, stared around, and pondered on her strange situation. She did not relish the prospect of being confined to four walls for an indefinite number of days. Going soon to Pressburg might be as long as her aunt's first promise of going soon to Castle Karpathy. Pray God neither Magda or her son turned out like Aunt Irma and Hugo! The very possibility of further betrayal sent Valerie shivering.

Then she became angry with herself. Useless to worry about two people whose integrity she had no reason to doubt. But she did wish Kaspar would return and tell her about his work and what place she was to have in this house. Was there any chance of him getting her to Hungary? But if it were true that her grandfather now said he would not receive her before she married Hugo... Oh, it was foolish to torment herself like this!

Valerie walked over to the bookcase and was about to look at its contents again when she noticed a space between the end of the case and the wall corner, and in this was wedged a large world globe. Use of the globe, otherwise geography, had been a subject at the boarding school for young ladies where she was educated. She enjoyed searching for different countries and now she prepared to do the same on this one, but first it must be pulled out of its confining space or she could not turn it round.

Unfortunately, Valerie did not realise the stand was broken. As she pulled, the globe itself fell on the floor with a loud clatter. She pushed back the stand, which was in two pieces and needed to be steadied by the wall and the bookcase, but then came the task of lifting the globe, which was very large. Valerie found it hard to grip the object, tried, but dropped it and this time the noise was even louder. She remembered with relief that the shop below was empty, so did not think she had disturbed anyone.

Here she was mistaken. One of the doors leading to the living-room opened and the sound of a voice made her jump in alarm.

'Who on earth are you? What are you doing here?'

The young man clad in bed-robe of blue brocade struck Valerie as the most arrogant person she had met. Of course he too must be a guest of Kaspar Webber. Perhaps there were others but they had not been awakened by the noise made by her clumsy efforts to retrieve the globe.

'What are you doing here?' he repeated.

She could hardly tell him to mind his own business.

'I was brought here by Frau Webber. Her

son is escorting her home—well, to where she is at present residing—and I was told to wait for Herr Kaspar's return. I am to be his guest and maybe help with some of his work.'

She could not explain what that help involved. She had expressed willingness to help in Kaspar's 'freedom' work, and to Valerie this personified fighting Prince Metternich's tyranny and furthering the ideals of Kossuth.

How critically was the young man staring at her. His cool gaze annoyed Valerie, though she could not explain why in actual words. She only knew she wanted to snub him and would take the first opportunity of doing so. This came after he enquired her name.

'As there is no-one present to introduce us, sir, I think you should be the first to reveal your identity.'

'Do you indeed! What airs and graces you are assuming for the daughter of an English commoner.'

'An English commoner! My father was a gentleman.'

'Born of trading stock with no claim to aristocratic blood, but he presumed to lift his eyes to a member of the ancient Karpathy family. Naturally he was regarded as an upstart Englishman.'

How dare he refer thus to darling Papa! With as much scorn as she could muster, Valerie said, 'You apparently take up the same attitude as did my grandfather when my mama and papa wished to marry.'

'It was a marriage not in accordance with your mother's social rank.'

'I don't acknowledge such ridiculous distinctions,' stormed Valerie. 'Papa and Mama were happy. I am proud to have had both as parents. You are more objectionable than Aunt Irma and Cousin Hugo.'

His identity was clear to her. She added, 'I conclude you are my Cousin Leonin, who has been missing for two years and is thought to have succumbed to danger from brigands or wolves in Russia, but was really a convict in Siberia after being charged with treason against the Tsar.'

'Who gave you this information, Cousin Valerie?'

'My aunt and Hugo. Some of it I learnt when I overheard a conversation between them.'

'Eavesdropping, eh?'

He made it sound as if she had done something wrong, thought Valerie. So this was the Cousin Leonin whose name had frequently been brought to her notice during the last few months.

'As you have somehow escaped from Siberia,' she said stiffly, 'you would be wise to show yourself without delay at Karpathy Castle. Aunt Irma is trying to convince our grandfather you are dead so that she can prevail upon him to name her as his heir.'

Leonin's contemptuous laugh irritated Valerie.

'This I know from Kaspar Webber's mother. I gather Aunt Irma can only inherit if a will is made in her favour.'

'Something Grandfather will never do because Aunt Irma is illegitimate. Her mother was far below him in rank and he never married her. You, child of a legitimate daughter, are heir after me, and then our distant cousins.'

'Me!'

The room was whirling round Valerie. So that was why her mother had never mentioned a sister. Even more important, she now saw why Aunt Irma was desperately anxious for her to marry Hugo. If Leonin was dead, or imprisoned in remote Siberia, Valerie was heir and the man who married her would gain Karpathy.

CHAPTER SIX

They tried to dupe me, was the thought that ran through Valerie's mind, swamping irritation against Leonin as she mused on Aunt Irma's and Hugo's scheme. The irritation returned when she saw he was still regarding her with an amused look, as if she had been a simpleton to accept the lies.

He said, 'So you really believed that Aunt Irma—and of course that includes Hugo—would inherit Karpathy once I was out of the way. I suppose Hugo has been proposing marriage to you. Now you understand why.'

'Indeed I do. All along I have been puzzled why he wanted to marry a penniless orphan, and why Aunt Irma encouraged him. It was quite obvious Hugo was not the least bit in love with me. He trades on his good looks, but he knew I was not swept away by them. He never charmed me.'

'Fortunate for you!'

Valerie looked sharply at her cousin. Did he think she was claiming immunity from Hugo's attractions because she was trying to conceal a broken heart? Surely not! Yet, somehow she felt he considered her a fool, and she hated his attitude of superiority.

Eager to change the subject she started to ask questions about his escape, that was not really an escape since, he told her, he had received the Tsar's pardon.

'But if you are a free man why are you keeping your return to this country a secret?'

'I came to Vienna with a band of gipsies, and disguised myself as one, hoping for the opportunity to observe Aunt Irma and plan revenge. That is still my objective, only I have pushed it aside because of a promise to help my old university friend, Kaspar Webber, in the work to which he is dedicated.'

'But our grandfather,' Valerie reminded him. 'Your first duty is to inform him that you are alive.'

'That can wait.'

'I don't think delay is wise, not with Aunt Irma plotting to obtain the estate and title. When I overheard that conversation between her and Hugo, she spoke about a will drawn up by some Tamas Szerb and how she hoped the old Count would sign it.'

'Tamas Szerb is Grandfather's Administrator.'

'Administrator of what?'

'Of the whole Karpathy estate—a kind of steward with legal training. He was always been a lackey to Aunt Irma, but even if he has drawn up a will naming her the heir Grandfather will never sign such a document.'

'I am sure she is plotting to inherit, which was why she had you sent to Siberia, for that was her doing through Prince Metternich's influence.'

'I have discovered that, Cousin Valerie, a long time ago, and although the property would legally pass to you, she could make sure of it for Hugo once you were his wife. You would not have been able to call your soul your own. That is, if you were allowed to live. As for Aunt Irma getting Tamas Szerb to draw up a will such as you describe! Was that before she knew about you?'

'I expect so,' said Valerie. Then she again urged her cousin to establish his claim straightaway. Her advice was spurned.

'My claim! But I am the heir. Until I marry and have a legitimate-born son, you come next, through your mother.'

'And Aunt Irma?'

'I keep telling you that she is a bastard. Grandfather has always treated her as such.'

'She is his daughter.'

'He has never liked her. She may have concocted grand schemes through Tamas Szerb after disposing of me—as she thought—but once you appear on the scene, you could inherit and her dear Hugo assume command of his wife's property . . . Oh, hello, Kaspar! You see your mother's protegée and I have become acquainted. It is interesting to meet a female cousin whose existence I knew nothing about until you informed me.'

'I have promised my mother to keep her hidden for the present. You and I have to go to Pozsony soon, and she can come with us. Mother thought that a good idea.'

'Pozsony is actually in Hungary, isn't it?'

'Yes, and Mother says you want to go to Hungary.'

'But to Karpathy Castle,' declared Valerie firmly.

She turned to Leonin, explaining she had written direct to the Count who replied by sending Aunt Irma to England to fetch her.

'I thought I was going straight to the Castle,' she went on. 'But there has been this delay in Vienna, presumably in accordance with Grandfather's wishes, only I doubt it.'

Then he suggested she help with Kaspar's work, as he was doing. Later, when he had finished, he would take her to confront their grandfather.

'He is an old man. He might die suddenly.'

'He won't. He is as strong as an old boar.'

'All the same...' but Valerie's protest was drowned by Kaspar talking about political schemes that were far more important to him than the private affairs of Leonin Karpathy and Valerie Gilliott.

The days that followed became increasingly boring for Valerie. While thankful to be hidden from Aunt Irma and Hugo, she hated confinement indoors especially as the weather was fine and springlike. The hours passed by so slowly.

The Webbers had a large and varied collection of books, and at first she was content to read and read, but she grew tired of this and there was nothing else to do. It was a relief when Magda appeared one evening and showed Valerie how to prepare the stew for supper. Kaspar, assisted by Leonin, had been doing this and he had refused Valerie's help on learning she was ignorant of cookery.

'Leonin says you taught him.'

'I don't want another pupil.'

Valerie did not offer again, nor did she ask to help with his freedom work, guessing that would be useless as he and Leonin seemed to conduct it through meetings they attended. Valerie, of course, dared not walk through the streets in case she by chance met Hugo, or one of her aunt's servants.

Magda's visits were rare since she was afraid of any absence being noted, and thus followed. So far she was sure her activities were unsuspected, but she exercised great caution. Valerie thought Magda was acting for her sake, but this was not entirely so. As an anti-Metternich spy, Magda was desperately anxious to retain a footing in the household through remaining Frau von Moricz's abigail, thus carefully watching her mistress's activities. Hugo did not interest her so much. He was lazy, she told Valerie, held a coveted government post due to Prince Metternich's influence, and did the minimum of work possible, while he was a noted womaniser.

'Well, what do he and Aunt Irma think about my disappearance?'

'Utterly mystified and very angry! Of course they are searching everywhere for you, but they can find no clue to your whereabouts. As your aunt holds your passport, she is confident you cannot leave Austria.'

'I never thought of that,' said Valerie, much alarmed. 'Therefore I cannot enter Hungary, can I? Kaspar has spoken of taking me to Pozsony when he is sent there.'

'That is arranged,' replied Magda in a triumphant tone. 'You can use mine, and if you wear a long cloak with hood shading your face, and maybe have a few wrinkles like mine painted on your cheeks, you will pass for a woman of my age.'

In this year of 1848, passports showed merely the holder's name and description.

'But how will you manage if Aunt Irma decides to go to Karpathy with you, and you have to cross the Hungarian border? Won't border police demand documents?'

'They will, but Frau von Moricz does not know I originally came from Germany, so had a passport. When we went to England, and it will be the same for Hungary, her passport had a blank for companion or maid. This is a usual practice and I shall travel to Hungary on hers without question. Yes, Kaspar and your cousin expect to be sent to Pozsony, and you will go with them. You will be safer from your aunt than in Vienna, and I still think you ought to approach your grandfather in person before she and Herr von Moricz do.'

'The letters he has sent Aunt Irma contain

very contradictory orders.'

'I wonder if any of them are genuine. He may not be aware of your existence.'

'He must, Magda. Originally I wrote direct to him. His first action was to send Aunt Irma to England for me.'

'Wasn't she staying at Karpathy Castle then?'

'I think so, but I don't really know. She said Grandfather showed her the letter. Could she have been lying? Only why?'

Magda could not help because she had not been to Karpathy or seen the old Count. However, owing to Irma von Moricz's habit of talking freely to Hugo in front of the abigail, as though the latter were part of the furniture, she thought her mistress had gone to Karpathy Castle at the request of 'a steward called Tamas Szerb.'

'What is he like?'

'I have no idea. Remember I was not appointed until your aunt came back from Hungary, dismissed Kataya, and advertised for another maid to accompany her to England. It is quite possible your letter never reached Count Karpathy, but was intercepted by this Tamas Szerb who communicated with Frau von Moricz. You see, it must have been a shock to learn of your existence, because you would inherit everything if, as she believed, she had got Herr Leonin out of the way.'

Confronting Count Karpathy seemed a

formidable prospect, whether Magda's conjectures were true or not. Leonin considered him a tyrannical grandparent as well as an autocratic landowner, describing him as hard, bitter, and unforgiving.

'Look how he banished your mother when she married beneath her station in life. It is a wonder he did not horsewhip your presumptuous father.'

'He threatened to do so. But Papa was not presumptuous. He was wealthy and his father had been a highly respected merchant.'

'Trade! Noble families of Hungary like the Karpathys do not marry into trading circles.'

Valerie did not trust herself to reply. She was furious with Leonin for clinging to beliefs in which he had been reared, yet he allied himself with a movement that was surely opposed to such nonsensical distinctions. Kaspar's father had not been a nobleman.

Ignoring Leonin's scornful remarks about her father, Valerie kept her temper and changed the subject, asking him about social conditions in Hungary among peasants and farmers. Here he displayed the influence of Kaspar that he had absorbed in university days. He keenly felt hatred of the old Count's treatment of peasantry, and it seemed his father—her dead Uncle Julius—had been equally harsh.

'When I am Count Karpathy, folk who labour for me shall be treated like human beings, not serfs. I see now that conditions in Hungary are nearly as bad as in Russia, and what I observed there when staying with my mother's people horrified me.'

'More so than your Siberian experiences?'

'Yes. Flogging is common and it is done with a cruel instrument called a knout. It was not until I went to the university and became friendly with Kaspar that I realised the injustice perpetrated by noblemen like my grandfather in Hungary, but it took Russia to convince me of the evils of a tyrannical government. That is why Kossuth is right when he says Hungary must be free from the Austrian yoke.'

Valerie had become dulled to the point of indifference to Kaspar's enthusiasm for his idol, Louis Kossuth. As for Leonin's inconsistent attitudes she found them equally trying and was glad to see less of him. The two men were out part of every day distributing leaflets, she was told, while during evenings, often well into the night, they were attending meetings of their fellow conspirators. Valerie expected to be asked to help, but Kaspar's mother told her son the girl must not go outside in case she were recognised, no matter how slight the danger.

It was easy for Leonin to disguise himself as a middle-aged man by putting on a false beard and wearing suitable clothes obtained for him.

'Couldn't I do something like that?'

'No, it is wiser for you to remain indoors

until we leave for Pozsony,' said Kaspar.

'When will that be?'

'When I receive orders to depart.'

Political events had hitherto meant little to Valerie, but now out of sheer boredom she tried to become more knowledgeable. Kaspar was too busy to answer her questions and she thought Leonin perversely unwilling. She did not realise what was going on in the innermost recesses of her cousin's mind. After her revelation of Aunt Irma's intrigues with Tamas Szerb, Leonin was racked by a desire to contact his grandfather and find out what was happening at Karpathy. However he had given an undertaking to Kaspar and he felt obliged to fulfil that promise first.

Hopes of something big about to happen came early in March when Louis Kossuth made a passionate speech in the Hungarian Diet, a speech that provoked excitement in Vienna as soon as news of its message arrived there. The Diet was a Hungarian body meeting at Pozsony, but with very limited power, although lately those powers were increasing.

Kaspar gave a report to Leonin and Valerie. 'He demands abolition of serfdom and dictatorship from Vienna, with the establishment of Hungary's independence, except that she will continue to accept the Austrian Emperor Ferdinand as her own king.'

'That sounds all right, but you've said over

110

and over again that Prince Metternich always persuades the Emperor to ignore anything the Diet proclaims.'

Surprised by Valerie's rejoinder, Kaspar took a second to recover himself sufficiently to explain that the new revolution in France had made tyrants like Metternich realise they had to think again before opposing lovers of freedom.

'But Kossuth is wisely making plans to recruit troops of his own—volunteers, who are to be called Honveds and secretly trained. They won't leave their homes in Hungary, but they can fight Austria if required. All this is very secret though, Valerie, and you must not speak about it to anyone outside.'

'I don't go outside, so I am hardly likely to do that.'

'Oh, you can discuss the scheme with Leonin.'

Discuss with Leonin! She wondered how interested he really was. This was a question she would not have asked herself even a week ago, but now she doubted his enthusiasm. He was becoming increasingly silent, as if his thoughts were elsewhere. She supposed he must be dwelling on his convict days in Russia, experiences one could not easily forget. At times he baffled her.

Valerie could not know how strictly the code of keeping a promise had been instilled in Leonin from childhood. Now he was finding his promise to Kaspar trying. He agreed with his friend's ideals and dutifully went with him to meetings, but he wanted action. Until there had been a successful rising, ousting Metternich and putting power into the hands of a democrat like Louis Kossuth, Leonin saw no chance of attending to his own affairs. He had come to Vienna with the overriding object of being revenged upon his aunt and cousin. He still wanted to accomplish that, but even more he was dreadfully homesick for the lands and castle he would one day own.

Karpathy Castle stood on a hill at the edge of an immense plain, a plain that had always held a deep fascination for him. Slicing vegetables in that dull kitchen, Valerie often watched and speculated on his thoughts, never guessing they were fixed on an imaginary horizon and galloping towards the ever-receding point of earth and sky. Vastness and silence seemed to possess the great Alfold, save where the traveller stumbled upon a tiny village like that of Karpathy. Leonin could fancy himself riding along a narrow dyke, with dark green swamp on one side and rich wheat-fields on the other, until he came in sight of the village church, of the inn known as a csarda, and the low built thatched cottages. Some day Karpathy would be his. Now he found he was longing for that time, although he had sufficient feeling for his grandfather not to wish the old man's days to be shortened prematurely. He wished the old man did not remain so feudal in his ideas. When Leonin became a nobleman, he told himself, he would not abuse his powers. Regarding Count Karpathy's anxiety about his safety, Leonin did not consider that, simply because he looked upon his grandfather as a man totally lacking in affection. At least that had been the boy's own experience. He experienced none himself, for his father was like the old Count, his mother had died when he was young, Aunt Lilla was a childish memory, and the bastard Aunt Irma treated like a superior maid until she made a satisfactory marriage, but even then it was beyond her power to ingratiate herself with these near blood relations. Leonin had never liked his aunt, and since her intrigues against him his mind was filled with the desire to be revenged on her and her son.

Now he had a female cousin as well. Valerie was just an additional obligation, for he would have to take her to Karpathy Castle when he could at last leave Kaspar for home.

Leonin's life hitherto had created in him a certain indifference to women. Some day he must marry suitably in order to carry on the line, but that was an obvious duty and, needless to say, he did not view the prospect in a romantic light. For sexual pleasure he had had his pick of peasant girls at Karpathy, then prostitutes in Vienna and Russia, but the mere exercise of sex quickly bored him. While attending Vienna University with Kaspar, he had flung himself into politics and, like Kaspar, had comparatively little to do with females. In Siberia he had no opportunity even if he had wanted one.

Valerie's experience of men was very limited. Her parents died before she was old enough to 'come out' in English society, while in Vienna she was positively guarded by Aunt Irma, who was determined Hugo should have no competitors. Fictional heroes, Valerie realised, were ideal creatures one did not encounter outside novels, but she could not regard Hugo as typical of real life men. She despised his insincerity, even more than his excessive drinking, and the attempt to rape her was terrifying.

Leonin was at least a gentleman. He would never behave so despicably, but she found him intolerably proud and she could not forgive him for scorning her darling father. He was even less companionable than the freedom-dedicated Kaspar. Oh, it was boring to be confined to a small house waiting to hear when the journey to Hungary would commence. She was not even doing anything constructive to further the rebellious underground movement. Kaspar took Leonin to meetings, but not her.

Then, on a sunny day at the beginning of March, everything was changed.

The two men had gone for an early stroll. She was dawdling over her toilette, wondering how she should get through the long day ahead, when her bedchamber door was flung open. Kaspar entered, handing her breeches, blouse, and cap—the usual garb of a workman. He was wearing the same.

'Hurry and get into these. You can pull the cap partly over one eye to hide your face. You must look like an artisan boy.'

'My aunt or my Cousin Hugo would recognise me.'

'They won't venture on the streets today if they are wise. It has started!'

'What has started?'

'The rising against Metternich and his tyranny. Now be quick. We must join the procession.'

A bewildered Valerie found herself in the Herrengasse, one of Vienna's widest streets, and with her were Kaspar and Leonin. Like themselves many of the marchers were clad in workmen's blouses and caps, and mingled with them could be seen some men in formal dress of black frock coat and top hat. They were university professors, Kaspar explained, but the bulk of the procession consisted of students shouting slogans and conspicuous by their gaily plumed hats.

On joining this purposeful crowd Valerie was almost carried along by the general excitement, which reached its height as they passed the Chancellery and abuse was yelled against Metternich.

'He will be compelled to resign,' remarked Kaspar.

'But where is the procession going?'

'To the Hofburg to deliver a petition to the Emperor himself.'

The pavements were crowded with spectators, mostly loudly sympathetic. People shouted encouragement until fear descended as marchers were faced by a wall of soldiers with drawn bayonets. Shots were fired to check progress.

'We can't have Valerie involved in a struggle,' Leonin told Kaspar.

Such was the note of authority in his voice that Kaspar obediently followed the other two, pushing a way through the scattering throng, only separating in a quiet side street.

'I can't desert my comrades. You take Valerie home and I'll join you later.'

But Magda's house was some distance and they had to dodge small bands of military who were stopping pedestrians and demanding to see papers. After avoiding a second such encounter, Leonin took Valerie in an inn.

'I used to come here often in university days, but they are long past and I shall not be recognised by the landlord. A mixed crowd always came here, so he won't think it unusual for two working men to drop in on a day of confusion like this.'

Actually Valerie had never been inside an inn. Although critical of the bare asphalt floor and scrubbed wooden tables with hard benches, she was impressed by the dwarf-sized orange trees in green boxes. Scattered all over the room, they gave an air of privacy as well as beauty. She could just see a girl sitting alone at the table next to the one selected by Leonin, and in spite of part concealment by a tree, it was clear she was heavily pregnant. The girl's face was unknown to Valerie who, however, was rendered uneasy by the way the stranger stared hard at her.

Leonin, without asking her preference, ordered a bottle of some special wine. He made no attempt at conversation while it was being served and glasses filled. Even though his thoughts were clearly elsewhere, Valerie was annoyed by his lack of courtesy. She enquired if the rising was likely to speed up Kaspar's mission—whatever its nature—to Pozsony.

'I am so anxious to get to Hungary. You ought to be the same. I am sure it is important for you to let our grandfather know you are alive, for goodness knows what Aunt Irma is plotting.'

'Our grandfather,' repeated Leonin in a jeering tone.

Valerie wanted to reply that the old Count

was indeed hers, although he had disowned her mother for marrying John Gilliott, but pride kept her from showing the indignation she felt. Instead she asked if the country round Karpathy was all part of the flat plain she heard was called the Alfold, and were there any towns near?

'To the west is Debrecen, and north is Miskolcz from where one soon reaches the Carpathian mountains. My father used to take me hunting among the lower slopes when I was quite a child.'

'Didn't he lose his life when hunting?'

Leonin nodded. 'Hunting wild boar in the wild forest land there, but I still love that part of my country, as well as the Alfold. The Carpathians always seem to me to represent Hungary's own spirit. They are stubborn and fearsome, but the setting sun embraces their outlines in a glow like a veil hiding that harshness. Hungary is a country with a tender heart. She has been at the mercy of tyrants—ancient Romans, infidel Turks, and now Austria, but soon she will be free. You know I have promised Kaspar to help her shake off the Austrian yoke, and I must keep that promise. In Kossuth, we have the leader for whom we have long been waiting.'

The impression Valerie received was that while wholeheartedly in agreement with Kaspar's ideals, Leonin really wanted to return to Karpathy because he so loved the place. On the other hand, his notions of the duties of a Hungarian estate owner differed completely from their grandfather's. He had said this before, also unashamedly expressed lack of affection for Count Karpathy.

Valerie did not think she should care for the old man either. He appeared to have treated Aunt Irma badly, and though Valerie hated her aunt the fact of being a bastard should not have been held against her.

It is no more her fault than Papa's trade origin.

Valerie was roused from her musings when Leonin remarked on the steady scrutiny of the girl sitting at the next table.

'But I don't know her. Do you?'

'Never set eyes on the female, and she isn't looking at me. It is you who interest her. Oh, she sees we have noticed so is trying to withdraw further behind that orange tree. My God! Look who has joined her.'

'Hugo! Then she must be the pretty abigail who was dismissed after the last visit to Karpathy and Magda took her place.'

'We're getting out of here,' muttered Leonin. 'This is not the time for a show-down with my vile cousin.'

But Hugo had risen from his seat. He faced Leonin and approached the other table through a space between two orange trees. Valerie could see he had gone deadly pale.

His voice quavered as he spoke.

'Where the hell have you come from?'

'Siberia, where you and Aunt Irma contrived to have me sent on a false charge from which I have now been cleared.'

'I want Valerie. She is in my mother's charge. I don't know what she is doing with you. We have looked everywhere for her.'

'But I happen to be head of the family in Grandfather's absence.'

Valerie was conscious that she was trembling. She knew she had been frightened of Hugo since the occasion he tried to rape her. In addition now she was scared of the pretty, sneering girl, who must be Kataya. Valerie had never seen her before, only heard her voice on the evening of her arrival in Vienna. The pregnancy was obvious and presumably the father-to-be was Hugo.

Other inn patrons were looking at the four. There was a round of applause as Leonin struck a blow at his cousin's shoulder, a blow so forcible that Hugo fell backwards against a table, then to the floor, just as if he had been shot. A screaming Kataya tried to help him to his feet. An agitated landlord appeared from the kitchen, but Leonin, seizing Valerie by the arm, hit the man, and before Valerie grasped what had happened she and Leonin had dashed through the kitchen and out of the back door. A bewildered cook-boy was the only person they encountered and he made no attempt to stop them.

Reaching the thoroughfare, they saw a small detachment of soldiers entering the buildings, including the inn, so Leonin dragged off Valerie from that street, up a side one, and then a maze of others.

'We must dodge Hugo. It would be fatal if he found where you and I are living.'

'We seem to be going in a different direction.'

'Be prepared for a long roundabout walk,' was all the consolation Valerie received.

She remarked that it was a pity he was not wearing the disguise of a beard, abandoned today when he put on workman's blouse and breeches, but Leonin declared that would not have fooled Hugo once they actually met. Ungraciously he added that it was the maid's recognition of Valerie that betrayed them, blame that Valerie considered most unfair.

CHAPTER SEVEN

They went along in silence after that, a silence broken by Valerie to ask how much further this detour would take them.

'If Hugo has recovered by now from the blow

121

you gave him, he cannot possibly find us, so do let us go home.'

'I am making for Kaspar's house now, through a whole quarter of poor dwellings. You have lost your sense of direction completely.'

'I know I have,' she agreed, and trying to sound agreeable she added that it was a joy to be out of doors after the long confinement in Magda's house.

She pointedly gave the correct name of the owner, but Leonin was not listening. That was obvious. He was concentrating on the various turnings. She knew he took a few wrong ones, then got back to the correct path, while all the time he was keeping a wary eye for possible patrolling soldiers or police. Whether the procession of rebels had succeeded in delivering their petition to the Emperor, or broken up and scattered, she had no idea.

Leonin's route went through almost deserted streets. Everyone must be in the centre of the city, near the Hofburg Palace. Kaspar was not at home. Nor was there any trace of a recent visit from Magda, but she would not dare, if able, to leave her abigail duties. It struck Valerie how boring they must be. When not actively attending to Aunt Irma's needs, Magda was supposed to sit in her cold poky bedchamber waiting a summons, but Valerie suspected there were frequent sorties as Magda listened outside doors trying to pick up possible information useful to Kaspar and his freedom organisation.

Versed in housekeeping by now, Valerie quickly produced a meal when they reached the house. Leonin ate with thoughts far away. His taking her service for granted, without a word of thanks, annoyed her. She would make him talk.

'Is this better fare than what you used to get in your Siberian prison?'

'I was first imprisoned in Russia proper—in St Petersburg—until sentence had been passed and I began the long journey east into Siberia. In the Fortress of Peter and Paul, rations were merely bread and water. The uncle who ultimately obtained my pardon was away in England then, and my mother's other relatives were too faint-hearted even to make enquiries about me. Not that I ought to blame them, for the tyranny of the Secret Police there is terrible. To ask questions about a suspect may mean one's own arrest. That is why I was so fortunate in having a courageous, powerful uncle, although his help came after I had been detained for nearly two years.'

'Aunt Irma and Hugo did not foresee that. I suppose Prince Metternich, at her request, denounced you to the Russian Secret Police. Is that the kind of regime he has here?'

'According to Kaspar, Austria and her dependent countries are governed by tyranny, but even Metternich's Secret Police can be nothing like the Russian, and there is no dreadful empty land dotted with convict establishments like Russia.'

'You mean Siberia, don't you? How were you taken there?'

'As a political prisoner I rode in a cart, but the ordinary criminals walked. Part of the journey was by boat, along rivers.'

'What kind of boats?'

'Large, barge type, each carrying about six hundred convicts. There is a great iron cage on deck and guards let up half the number at a time to get air, for it is confoundedly stuffy below. Oh, food was slightly better, but this was what I was compelled to endure, and by then I had discovered that Aunt Irma, through the Austrian Chancellor, was responsible for the false information laid against me. I shall never forgive her!'

He looked almost murderous as he said this, and while Valerie was shocked by such cold, bitter anger, she could hardly blame him. Still curious, she asked what it was like when he reached his prison destination in Siberia.

'It wasn't a prison in the ordinary sense, for we lived in a camp and there were no bolts or bars on doors.'

'You mean you were not locked up?'

'There was no need. The whole land is a vast prison—desert to the south and vast forests on the other sides. And the winter is so severe that though many prisoners run away during the summer, cold and starvation force them to return in autumn, if not caught by natives.'

'Are there natives?'

'Yes, they live in villages, and a few towns. I was taken to work at Irkutsk, a large commercial centre, for a time, and of course guarded and shackled—yes, shackled then! Not that natives would help an escaping convict. They prefer to hand him to the authorities for the substantial money reward they will receive. I soon found any chance of freeing myself was hopeless. Once on the western side of the Urals, if I had been lucky enough to get so far, I should have been arrested because I had no permit to travel. The Russian regime is frightful! I thought treatment of the peasantry appalling when I was an honoured guest of my mother's family. It is far worse than Hungary, although Grandfather is a tyrant.'

'You were lucky to have this uncle who did secure your freedom,' said Valerie. 'It is something Aunt Irma can never have foreseen.'

'She thought I was out of the way for good, so somehow—though God knows how—she would push Hugo into line for the inheritance of Karpathy. But she will certainly have a shock when Hugo tells her how he met me today in Vienna.'

'Surely you ought to go to Karpathy without
125

delay, Leonin, and acquaint Grandfather with the true situation.'

'I promised Kaspar first to help him.'

Leonin's mouth shut in an obstinate line that Valerie had observed before. What a determined person he was, and a selfish one!

At last Kaspar came in, an excited triumphant Kaspar.

'Here you are! Thanks for looking after Valerie, Leonin, but I am sorry you missed all the excitement. Yes, there was a scrap with the military and a few demonstrators were hit, though not seriously. The soldiers were obviously half-hearted about carrying out orders. They pushed people back, and chased a few, threatened their bayonets, but did not use them. You could tell where their sympathies lay. And when the crowd reached Metternich's Palace, they contented themselves with guarding entrances.'

'Did Metternich appear on the balcony?'

'And risk his own neck—no fear! There was a rumour he had gone to the Hofburg to see the Emperor, then to the Archduke Franz Charles.'

'He is a military man, isn't he?'

Kaspar nodded, continuing his story with a description of how the procession surged to the Hofburg Palace and finally managed to have their petition presented to the Emperor Ferdinand, a weak man who suffered from attacks of epilepsy and usually relied upon his

126

chancellor, Prince Metternich.

'Did the Emperor receive the petition favourably?'

'Yes, especially as the Archduke Louis put in a request for Metternich's resignation.'

'Will Metternich give it?'

'He has been compelled to do so, and before I left my friends there was another rumour, this time one that he had scuttled out of Vienna and hidden in a washerwoman's cart while his carriage went ahead, empty, for him to join in the country. He will certainly flee from Austria. He knows his day of power is over. Anyway, Vienna is celebrating his downfall by putting candles in windows of houses to light in triumph after dark.'

'There won't be any candles in the windows of Aunt Irma's house,' remarked Valerie. 'She won't be able to continue her spying activities now she no longer has her friend and protector. Perhaps she and Hugo will go to Hungary.'

But Kaspar took no interest in Frau von Moricz, not even whether Magda would continue her service as abigail, or not. Leonin enquired their next move, and his friend eagerly proclaimed it.

'I have been assigned the duty of going immediately to Pozsony to acquaint Kossuth and the Hungarian Diet with the marvellous news. Of course you two will come with me. I need Leonin and I promised Mother not to desert Valerie.'

'I am willing to help,' said Valerie, but her offer was ignored.

Kaspar continued, 'The roads out of the city may have soldiers marching to take up extra guard at the frontiers, and pro-Metternich supporters may be fleeing, so my comrades think it better for me to go by boat.'

'Will that be easier when there is such confusion?'

'An easier way to avoid attracting attention, especially as I have found a pro-Kossuth captain who only deals in cargo, not passengers.'

'But we are not cargo.'

'Don't fuss, Valerie.' Kaspar had long ceased to address her as Fraulein or Miss. 'You will be hidden while Leonin and I pretend to be crew.'

'Anyway, I have your mother's passport. Does she know about this move?'

'Impossible to contact her. I shall leave a note here. Of course we may be back soon.' He added, 'You can't take much baggage.'

Valerie said nothing but she was determined once she got inside Hungary to remain there. She found the river journey rather uncomfortable in the cramped hiding-place assigned to her. Once the boat stopped and the sweat poured down her face in alarm. Was another vessel coming beside them? They had certainly stopped at some unexpected place, for she heard the shouting of orders and men coming aboard, but whatever they wanted she was not discovered, and within an hour they were on their way again.

Some time after this the door of the cupboard, where she was concealed, was opened and Leonin informed her that they were safe in Hungarian waters, having passed through the Austrian frontier without detection. At dawn they reached Pozsony. Leonin seemed to know the town well. He proudly pointed out its chief buildings to Valerie and showed her the hill up which kings of Hungary had to ride when crowned, taking an oath to defend the country from all enemies.

'An empty promise now,' he said in a tone full of disillusionment.

He went on, 'Pozsony is really the capital of Hungary, but that counts for nothing now, although it should do with Metternich gone, because Kossuth will be able to claim real power for the Diet. You will find yourself in love with the town if we stay long. Unfortunately, as in Vienna, everybody speaks German, not Magyar.'

'I ought to learn the Magyar language.'

'I'll teach you a little,' came his unexpected offer.

Valerie asked if Magyar was spoken at Karpathy.

'The peasants know no other tongue. It is the same with lower servants at the Castle.

129

Otherwise German, or French, is used. Noblemen and their families affect to despise all things Hungarian.'

'Do you think our grandfather will refuse to accept me when I arrive?'

'You are wasting your time if you go to Karpathy.'

Leonin's crushing declaration only increased Valerie's resolve.

'I intend to see him. For one reason, I am penniless. He can hardly let me starve. Then this tale of Aunt Irma about him not receiving me until I am married to Hugo must be false. Do you think she was also lying when she said he sent her to England for me after reading my appeal letter—Grandfather, I mean? Neither he nor she was aware of my existence before the letter came.'

Another possibility was brought forward by Leonin, one that had previously been suggested by Magda.

'Perhaps Grandfather never had your letter. It could have been intercepted by Tamas Szerb, who is Aunt Irma's uncle as well as steward and always ready to assist her—secretly, of course. The news would wreck any plans she had after disposing of me. Aunt Lilla's daughter, a very unwanted niece, was the next heir. Not that Aunt Irma as a bastard ever had any chance.'

'She seemed to think she could get a will signed in her favour. That was when she

130

believed you would never get out of Siberia so could be presumed dead, while my existence was unknown.'

'I am surprised she could entertain such a delusion, even with that rascally Tamas Szerb's help, but she will do anything for Hugo and it was his ultimate benefit that counted with her. But how absurd when Grandfather had always sneered at Aunt Irma because she was a bastard.'

'Considering he was responsible for her birth, he had no right to treat her with scorn.'

'But he did, and he always will.'

'Leonin, do you really think it possible that our grandfather might not have seen my letter, so does not yet know I exist?'

'I think that is highly probable. All the tale of Grandfather sending her to England for you was a pack of lies.'

'Well, what can I do?'

'When I have discharged my duty to Kaspar, I will go to Karpathy taking you with me, and we will confront Grandfather together.'

The second time Leonin had shown any inclination to help his cousin!

Their stay in Pozsony turned out to be a brief one, for very soon Kaspar was ordered, by whoever locally controlled his actions, to travel to Pest, the large and important commercial city lying further down the Danube. Kossuth had plans for the Hungarian Diet to be moved there after he had been to Vienna and had a personal interview with the apparently yielding monarch. Meanwhile, as communications were poor and news travelled slowly, Kossuth was anxious the pro-Magyar Pest should learn about the rising in the Austrian capital and be urged to take similar action. People there must defy the police. They must proclaim their desire for liberty.

Valerie thought that she was gradually getting further east, though slowly, and she willingly left Pozsony, again by boat. Leaving that town behind she leaned against the deck rail, hoping for inspiring scenery, but so far that on the river banks was flat and dull, its monotony only broken by large herds of cattle.

Leonin had become friendlier since they were within Hungarian boundaries. Now he came and stood beside her, talking about Pest and emphasising that it was a predominantly Magyar community.

'Although you will see a variety of other races, like Jews, Wallachs, Czechs, all wearing distinctive dress. As spring advances, the Zeugen-volk, whom you call Gipsies, will be drifting back from the south.'

Pest lay on one bank of the Danube. On the opposite side was the ancient city of Buda, but this was strongly Austrian orientated.

'A bridge is being built to connect the two places, but it won't be completed for another year, so at present crossing has still to be made by boats in summer and sledging over the ice in winter.'

As they approached, Valerie remarked that Buda looked far more impressive than Pest, for the latter was low-lying whereas the buildings of Buda stretched upwards, culminating with a citadel and a royal palace. Leonin explained what these were, and how the Empress Maria Theresa built the palace, and that the plateau on which it stood was some eight hundred feet above the river.

'But Buda is Austrian in soul,' he said with scorn. 'Pest is truly Hungarian.'

They landed at Pest and immediately Kaspar took them on foot to the centre of the city. Valerie asked where they were going to lodge.

'I'll find somewhere before dark, but first I have to spread news of Vienna's rising. Here are cockades for you and Leonin to wear. You see they are tri-coloured. By tomorrow everybody in Pest will vaunt one.'

He pinned one on his own shoulder while his two companions did the same. A puzzled Valerie was about to ask their significance when Kaspar began shouting to passers-by, 'Rise, Magyars, rise!'

In no time he had attracted a crowd and was telling them of how a petition had been accepted by the Emperor who was at last getting rid of the oppressive Prince Metternich.

'What Vienna has done, you citizens of Pest and every Hungarian town must follow. See these cockades of red, white, and green ribbon. What do the colours represent? Liberty, Equality, Fraternity!'

It began to rain and people put up their umbrellas. A man held one over Valerie's head and, as she clung to Leonin terrified they would be separated, she found they were being swept along by a powerful avalanche of humans moving in a mass towards the town hall. She did not know what the building was until enlightened by Leonin, who understood Magyar and heard those around saying a proper assembly must take place in the dry. They must hear again what Vienna had achieved and decide on their own course of action.

Leonin detached her from the umbrella escort and secured both her and himself standing places on the platform. There was no room to sit, but the platform was less suffocating than the main body of the hall which was crammed with people. A band of musicians had somehow got inside with their instruments, and they began to play a forbidden revolutionary tune, the Rakoczy march.

The experience of being in a crowd, and a crowd aflame with fervour, was something entirely new to Valerie. She was somewhat scared, though trying to suppress fears and imbibe courage from the coolness of Leonin.

But was he heart and soul with the crowd?

In spite of supporting Kaspar's ideals, Valerie felt that, unlike the rest of those listening to Kaspar's eloquence, Leonin's thoughts had strayed to Karpathy and how he meant to improve the peasants' lot there when he became count. She had not previously realised what a burden it was for him to put off his visit to his home.

Rise, Magyars, rise! Although the words were in a language strange to her, yet she knew what the oft-repeated phrase meant. Otherwise she understood nothing of what Kaspar was saying, and he went on and on until interrupted by someone shouting in a loud stentorian voice for the release of some revolutionary imprisoned at Buda. He used German which was immediately translated by a friend who appeared ashamed that anything but the Magyar language was being spoken.

And I shall collapse if all this does not end soon, thought Valerie, conscious only of her need for food and bed. But she had to endure another two hours before an elderly man, who was on the platform and seemed to be regarded with respect, caused Kaspar to cease by bringing forward other speakers, and a pale-faced young man addressed the meeting. A couple of others, summoned by the elderly man, helped to conduct the three visitors through the crowd to a lodging. It consisted of only two rooms, one a bedchamber which was allotted to Valerie. The place was rented by a young poet, the man now addressing the meeting, and when it ended he would go to a friend's. In the meantime there was at least cold meat and coarse bread to eat.

The elderly man sat at the table too, but he talked while they ate, and as he spoke in Magyar, Valerie had no idea what he said, but she noticed Kaspar looked pleased and there was an air of approval about Leonin.

'What is to happen next?' she boldly asked Kaspar when the three were alone.

'You should go to bed at once, Valerie. There is a room for you. Leonin and I will manage on chairs in here.'

'I gathered that was the arrangement, but surely it is only for tonight. We need more accommodation than this.'

'Remember our arrival was unexpected. We are fortunate to have this.'

'But after tonight?'

'Tomorrow we catch an early train to Szolnok.'

'Where is that?'

'Over a hundred miles from Pest.'

'In the east of Hungary?'

'Yes, then we go to Debrecen, then to towns nearer the Carpathians. I have been assigned two important duties, to raise money and men for our cause.'

'But I thought the cause was won.'

'Alas we are dealing with a weak ruler. The Emperor may break his word. Metternich may try to return and be successful. No, when I saw Kossuth at Pozsony he feared blood would be shed before true independence could be secured for Hungary. For fighting he needs what I must obtain through personal appeals, especially recruitment.'

'In Vienna you spoke about Kossuth's plan for volunteers and that the men would be called Honveds, only you impressed secrecy upon me then.'

'There is no need for secrecy now. My word, Valerie, you take in more than one expects. I mean you look so dreamy.'

'How far is Szolnok from Karpathy?'

'We could go there on the way to Debrecen,' said Leonin. 'The railway ends at Szolnok so we shall have to continue in a horse-drawn vehicle, or actually riding. Can't that be arranged, Kaspar? It would not be wasting time because funds for Kossuth might be obtained from the Count, my grandfather.'

'You say he is a reactionary,' exclaimed Valerie. 'He would surely oppose help to Kossuth.'

Kaspar remarked that the purpose of the money need not be disclosed. Valerie said that would be deceitful, and Leonin turned on her in a most aggressive fashion.

'Who are you to dictate what Kaspar and I should do? As a matter of fact all my mother's jewellery lies locked up at the Castle and it already belongs to me so I can take that if I wish. When I said we would go there I did not include you, for I am positive you will not be received. Grandfather has never forgiven your mother.'

What right had Leonin to bring up this elopement of her darling mother and marriage with a commoner! Valerie turned away angrily from him. She did not remind him that he had promised to take her and confront their grandfather together. She had begun to feel that this cousin of hers was rather a nice person after their friendly intercourse during the journey from Vienna to Pest, and in Pest. Now annoyance over his haughtiness, and the fact that he despised her as child of a non-aristocratic father, was uppermost in her mind, and she longed to tell him so. But during those dreadful governess days Valerie had learnt the value of holding her tongue. She kept silent now, for she would need Leonin's help at Karpathy. She was certainly going there, but she required him to acquaint the old Count with her arrival. And supposing her grandfather did refuse to allow her to enter the castle?

CHAPTER EIGHT

A train journey was in itself an exciting experience for Valerie, who had only travelled that way when Aunt Irma was bringing her from England to Vienna. She looked forward to seeing the Hungarian countryside as the train left Pest, but it was a dreary wet day and she saw nothing to give her an adequate impression. To make matters worse she broke her resolution against retorting when Leonin made deprecating remarks about her father's people being in trade. The result was a quarrel which left the two on very cold terms.

Only one subject was uppermost in Kaspar's mind, namely forwarding the cause for which Kossuth stood. He had been supplied with the address of a priest who would give the three hospitality during their short stay in Szolnok. He turned out to be a chubby-faced, amiable man, and his presbytery was a pleasant dwelling where Valerie felt they were welcome. She was delighted to see a large collection of books, including such unlikely ones as the novels of Sir Walter Scott in English, and she could have passed a few days just reading, but she was determined not to be left out of activities as she had been in Vienna.

She firmly told Kaspar, 'I want to help, and

as there is no danger of my meeting Aunt Irma or Hugo, you must permit me to come along with you.'

He willingly consented and Leonin was forced into sulky acquiescence. The three distributed leaflets, held meetings, first with the priest's own flock, then with wider audiences. Finally they attended a local fair, held at Szolnok for three days annually.

Valerie had been impressed by the peasants' clothes worn in the town, which she gathered were truly Hungarian and characteristic of the Alfold plain region. Men wore wide trousers made of coarse white linen, and their shirts were too thin to dispense with heavy sheepskin cloaks fastened with large brass clasps. Women's skirts were puffed out by masses of petticoats, and they favoured gaily-patterned blouses decorated with ribbons. Again, they needed shawls as a protection against the spring wind.

Soon Valerie began to notice general wearing of the red, white, and green cockades, signs of support for Hungarian independence, and brought in quantity by Kaspar. He and his two helpers also vaunted them, besides flourishing sticks from which floated linen in the same three colours, a kind of makeshift flag. This was daring action when submission to Austrian rule had for long cowed the population. Now there was definite defiance of the authorities, who suddenly seemed to have lost any power to intervene.

The fair attracted crowds from far and near. Besides townsfolk and peasants, Valerie saw a set of gipsies, and the last-named fascinated her as she watched them endeavouring to sell their home-made wares while many of the gipsy women were earning money by telling fortunes. She wished she could have her future predicted, as, for instance, the chances of her grandfather accepting her.

As ordered by Kaspar she wandered among the crowd, distributing cockades to those not wearing the insignia of liberty, but on the whole these tri-coloured ribbon badges were accepted with enthusiasm. By now she had acquired a few Magyar phrases, enough to explain, parrot-fashion, for what the cockades stood. It was the priest who really helped her, Kaspar being so absorbed in his own efforts at propaganda.

He doesn't really need either of us, was Valerie's conclusion. She was increasingly impatient to reach Karpathy and for Leonin to show himself there. The promise made to Kaspar about putting work for Kossuth before personal matters was, in her opinion, wrong, for they were to cut out Karpathy when going to Debrecen.

She gazed fascinated at one of the food stalls, kept by Hungarian peasants, not gipsies. It was

141

piled high with loaves of freshly baked black bread. There were strings of sausage, long strips of red peppered bacon, and jars of pickled gherkins. Next to it was a smaller one selling honey cakes and gingerbread that looked so appetising she wished she had money to buy some, although the three strangers were well-fed at the priest's house.

She turned to another stall where rugs, sheepskin coats, and silk handkerchiefs were being sold. With a shower of rain starting, the woman in charge flung a shawl over her head, but Valerie moved into a covered part of the fair ground and looked at pipes and tobacco, both much favoured by the Hungarians who were greatly addicted to smoking. Looking at goods for sale made Valerie feel regret that she knew so little about her mother's homeland. Mama had told her nothing because Papa wanted the country where he was insulted to be pushed out of mind.

This country fair gave Valerie a strange sense of belonging to Hungary. Her previous life in England had receded in memory and was now the foreign country. She was certain her future lay here.

'Oh, there you are, Valerie. Leonin has met some gipsies he knew at Karpathy. The tribe continues to go there every year and are on their way there now.'

'Do you mean to say Leonin associates with

gipsies?'

'He does with these,' said Kaspar. 'He knows gipsy ways and plays one of their instruments, the czimbalom.'

'Of course! Now I remember he was the czimbalom player in that orchestra hired by Baron Beckmann in Vienna. You passed him a note which he could read and I was so surprised. The little I had heard of gipsies—well, surely they have no education?'

'Not as a rule, although when the Empress Maria Theresa reigned she tried to improve their lot. Then there is a cranky landowner in Transylvania who interests himself in their welfare, but generally the Zeugen-volk have no learning except their own lore. I believe the tribes vary. These whom Leonin has met here are obviously superior to the rough specimen he took refuge with in Vienna.'

'Oh, he took refuge with them! Why?'

'Some mad notion of getting an opportunity to watch your relations who had condemned him to Siberia. He intends to have his revenge one day.'

'Kaspar,' said Valerie, detaining him by the arm. 'You must release Leonin from that promise to put off returning to Karpathy before he has helped you with recruiting enough Honveds and obtaining money to support Kossuth. Regarding money, remember he is prepared to sell valuable jewellery left him by his mother, and give you the proceeds.'

'Leonin need not keep a promise if he finds it inconvenient.'

'But he feels he must, out of loyalty to the friendship that exists between you both.'

'He has not asked me to release him from his promise.'

Kaspar sounded very stiff. He was clearly vexed, but Valerie persevered.

'Of course he would not ask you such a thing. He has great belief in the work you have undertaken, and he has the same progressive ideas, but I can see that inwardly he longs to go to his old home. Now we are so near the place he ought to take advantage of the opportunity, and once there he is not going to find it easy to leave.'

In an off-hand tone of voice, Kaspar said, 'I plan to leave Szolnok the day after tomorrow and go straight to Debrecen. I cannot afford to waste my time on a reactionary Hungarian nobleman such as Count Karpathy.'

'It won't be a waste of time for Leonin. Let him and me leave you, because it is important for me to see my grandfather, though not so important as for Leonin.'

Another thought struck Valerie.

'We may have news of your mother. Frau von Moricz may arrive, because her spying for Metternich must be ended, and your mother as her abigail would come with her. Leonin could hear anything important she has heard and send you word, or he could put Frau Webber in touch with you. Please Kaspar!'

'There is a good deal in what you say,' he admitted grudgingly.

They strolled along and found Leonin talking to some male gipsies, one of the group being quite well-dressed in a blue coat with gold buttons and a heavy gold chain round his neck. He certainly did not look poverty-stricken in accordance with Valerie's first ideas about these folk, and not altered by the showy costumes provided by Baron Beckmann at his party.

Kaspar noticed Valerie's eyes fixed on the particular gipsy.

'That is the leader,' he explained. 'I heard Leonin call him the Volvode, and they appear to have been formerly acquainted. I wonder if your haughty grandfather knew his grandson had gipsy friends in secret and probably helped them. If you want evidence that Leonin is not like the usual Hungarian aristocrat, there it is.'

'All the more reason why Leonin should concentrate on Karpathy, not give up his time to your mission. By each going his own way, you will both help Kossuth better, and when he does become the chief power in Hungary he will be thankful to have at least one loyal subject among the aristocracy. In fact it will be two if I am allowed to stay indefinitely at my mother's old home.'

'I doubt if you will be,' was Kaspar's discouraging reply. 'Leonin does not think so.'

Valerie pursed her lips. She would test the matter herself, not heed Leonin's damning words.

Leonin now detached himself from the gipsy group and came to the others, suggesting they found a refreshment booth where they could have a meal. He would treat them, he declared. This was an invitation Valerie had no scruples about accepting. She was still without a single coin in her purse, while she had discovered Leonin left Russia well supplied with funds through the noble relative who secured his release. Valerie was inclined to think Kaspar sponged on her cousin, but Kaspar was intent on saving the money which his Kossuth comrades in Vienna had put at his disposal for journeying about Hungary doing the work assigned to him.

The shower had ceased some time ago and the afternoon turned out fine and mild. They found a refreshment booth just outside a tent with tables on the edge of a wide expanse of grass. Leonin explained there would be dancing there and they should be able to watch it as they ate. In the background were braziers on which food was cooked. He ordered gulyas, a stew highly peppered and they also had potatoes mixed with red pepper and sour cream. For wine he said Valerie must have a mild variety, not the strong spirit called slivovitz which Kaspar wanted.

They had just finished the stew and were drinking from a second bottle of wine when a gipsy band appeared and began to play what was at first a sweet, lilting tune. They then changed to wild, passionate music, that Leonin explained was the csardas, the national dance of Hungary.

'Come Valerie, we'll join in.'

'But I don't know the dance. I shan't be able to do the steps.'

'Oh, you will if you follow the beat. I'll guide you.' Intoxicated by the compelling rhythm, Valerie found herself moving in harmony with Leonin to the strange, and now slow, music. She did not question whether or not the dance was still the csardas. She was only conscious of her cousin's bodily nearness and the protective happy feeling this proximity gave her.

The tempo quickened and Valerie's steps became uncertain. Leonin was vexed at her blunderings and she pleaded to join those watching.

'You have danced these gipsy measures again and again. I am spoiling your enjoyment by my clumsiness.'

He did not deny this and the silent acquiescence hurt, although it was justifiable. She was left standing beside a group of gipsy women whose chanting in an unknown tongue

147

added charm to the playing of instruments by the band. The czimbalom was offered to Leonin and Valerie fully expected him to take it, but he shook his head. Instead he led one of the singers to join in the dance.

The woman had the usual long black hair and bold black eyes. She was not pretty in any sense of the word, but her body swayed in unison with Leonin's as the musical speed increased. Standing and watching, Valerie was fascinated by the changing scene, but especially by Leonin and his partner. Their performance affected every nerve of her body and in imagination she too was dancing. It was the same with two succeeding women whom Leonin partnered. She was also very envious of their skilful performances.

It was a surprise to Valerie when Leonin ceased to dance and came to stand by her.

'Watch carefully,' he said. 'The zarabardas is next, and of course it will be a solo.'

'Zara—what?'

'Zarabardas, the snake dance.'

In imitation of a serpent coiling and uncoiling, the gipsy's body swayed sensuously, as though preparing to strike at a prey, while the music now sounded passionate and irresistibly seductive.

Its effect hypnotised Valerie whose previous experience of seeing gipsy women dance was when their performance had shocked the guests at the party in Vienna. What would those fashionably conventional people have thought of this display in which every movement was calculated to rouse exciting emotions? Yet were those individuals as restrained as they pretended, or really so moral? On what terms were Aunt Irma and Prince Metternich? As for Hugo he was undoubtedly a libertine. The memory of his one display of physical passion caused Valerie to shudder.

It brought too a consciousness that the physical contact between husband and wife would not be abhorrent if love were present. She would welcome embraces from Leonin while she had loathed Hugo's. Had she fallen in love with Leonin? No, that was ridiculous.

I was just influenced by dancing with him, Valerie decided, moving her lips to repeat again and again an emphatic 'No.' Then she endeavoured to give her whole attention to the wild snake dance, but its spell no longer held her. Instead, practical considerations of the present situation gripped her.

Leonin was being very foolish in keeping that absurd promise to Kaspar. He knew this particular set of gipsies well, so why did he not travel with them to Karpathy? He could use his influence for her to go too. Valerie did not stop to consider that the gipsy mode of life might not suit her. Her mind was fixed on Karpathy and the importance of the old Count being made

149

aware that his grandson and heir was alive, before Aunt Irma tried to carry out her diabolical schemes.

They were diabolical towards Leonin, she reflected. And her aunt had obviously tried to use her to further Hugo's chances. Yet Valerie still did not know whether Count Karpathy knew of her existence, or not. That she had to discover. She could certainly remedy any ignorance by appearing at the Castle, and that she must do in spite of Leonin declaring she would not be welcomed. Without money, without friends, and in a strange country, help from her grandfather was a necessity, and if she were actually in his presence surely he could not turn her adrift.

The snake dance ended among enthusiastic applause. Leonin stepped forward to congratulate the dancer. Valerie looked round for Kaspar. He had left them after the meal. The fair ground was crowded and had numerous other attractions, such as bobbing for oranges, and monstrosities on show. Valerie did not pause to look at a Giant or a Fat Woman, but persevered in her search until she spotted Kaspar on the far side of the crowd talking earnestly with the keeper of a bored-looking bear, and giving the man the usual cockade and sheet, which she guessed he would be unable to read.

Determined to talk to him again Valerie

followed in the direction Kaspar had taken, but was annoyed by the attention of various men. She knew she looked different from the local girls, and, in any case, a lone female was unusual and considered fair game. Valerie was at a further disadvantage through understanding only a smattering of Magyar. If she had spoken German these strangers might have been less bold, but she only showed by angry gestures how she resented their approaches.

She managed to rebuff them until she was accosted by one who was elderly, and he positively refused to leave her. He was fair and dapper, and had cunning light grey eyes that held the same expression of desire she once saw in Hugo's. There was also curiosity, as if the man wanted to probe into her identity. He began to ask questions in Magyar, then changed to German. She did not answer but shook her head and tried to escape from him. None of the crowd took any notice. If a well-off man fancied a pretty girl who was foolish to go unescorted, it was none of an outsider's business.

'Surely you do not belong here, Fraulein?'

Unable to ignore him any longer, Valerie said she was in Szolnok on a visit to friends.

'And you have lost them in this crowd. Permit me to have the privilege of assisting your search for them.'

'No, thank-you,' said Valerie firmly.

She wished she could conquer the trembling

151

in her legs, but she was badly frightened and it was with great relief that she saw the tall figure of Leonin pushing through the throng of people. The elderly man was so engaged in making passionate requests to conduct Valerie to her friends that he did not notice Leonin's advance. Valerie was about to rush to her cousin when Leonin backed and vanished from view.

'What is the matter, pretty Fraulein? Have you seen someone you know?'

'He is over there and waiting for me,' she lied.

Why on earth had he gone like that? Didn't he realise this stranger was pestering her? Now she was desperate to shake off the nuisance. Facing the man boldly, she said, 'Kindly leave me.'

That he had no intention of doing. Valerie was sickened by the leering expression on his shiny face, as well as by glittering eyes that seemed to pierce through clothing to her flesh. Memories concerning that horrible ordeal with Hugo returned to her, and she feared a repetition, for the people around were obviously indifferent to how a well-dressed man behaved to a lone girl.

Now he was touching her cheek with a moist hand, and the action made her shudder. He would try to kiss her next.

Thank God! Here was Kaspar come to her rescue.

The libertine staggered from a blow delivered straight at his chest, rendering him breathless, and a second later Valerie found Kaspar was speedily dragging her away. It was not until they reached the presbytery that she saw Leonin who had preceded them there.

Valerie's annoyance at his desertion could not be suppressed.

'You saw me in company with that horrible stranger, and it must have been obvious he was taking advantage of my unprotected position, but you walked away instead of coming to my rescue. If Kaspar had not turned up . . .'

She could not say what she had really feared.

'I came at Leonin's request,' said Kaspar. 'He did not want to be seen by that man.'

'Why not?'

Leonin gave a barely perceptible sneer, but sneer it was.

'You are always so clever, my dear Cousin Valerie. However, you do not know you were talking to a creature I particularly want to avoid, and so should you.'

'Who was he then?'

'None other than Tamas Szerb, my grandfather's Administrator of whom I told you, if you remember.'

'Yes indeed, and of course I would not willingly have spoken to such a creature, who is scheming against us both.'

'I will protect my own interests,' said Leonin coldly.

Kaspar broke in.

'Because Leonin wishes to reach Karpathy quickly tomorrow he is hiring a chaise. He did consider going with the gipsies, but they travel too slowly.'

'I am going in that chaise too,' declared Valerie.

Leonin said with marked unwillingness, 'I suppose I shall be obliged to take you with me. You can wait in the village while I make sure our grandfather will receive you.'

Valerie could see he was thoroughly out of humour. He hated her determination, and having to give way to it, but there was something else she felt sure, and of this she became aware when Kaspar left them.

Leonin turned angrily towards her.

'How dare you interfere with my private affairs?'

'What do you mean?'

'I had given my word to Kaspar that I would not attend to these matters until we had both spread the freedom message widely. Now he has released me from that bond.'

'Aren't you pleased? It is urgent that you go to Karpathy. You have said you wanted to go, not only to thwart Aunt Irma's schemes, but to be revenged on her for getting you sent to Siberia.'

'Maybe,' acknowledged Leonin. 'Only I happen to regard keeping my word of honour as more important.'

'I am sure Kaspar prefers you to settle matters at Karpathy first. That is what he has told you, hasn't he?'

'Yes, owing to your interference. You had the audacity to plead with him on my behalf, and I resent that. In future, leave me to manage my own affairs, Cousin Valerie.'

CHAPTER NINE

The following morning Valerie took her seat in the hired chaise which Leonin was going to drive. He appeared quite used to this type of Hungarian vehicle, with its accommodation limited to two people and drawn by three horses.

They set off at a brisk pace that became even faster when they were out of Szolnok. There had been a friendly parting with Kaspar when Leonin promised to ride to Debrecen with the jewellery he was giving for the Kossuth movement. Kaspar would be in that town to receive it in another week, and intended to stay at Debrecen at least a month.

Privately Valerie thought Kaspar could have travelled by way of Karpathy and saved Leonin the journey, but she was glad Leonin did not wait for Kaspar's departure from Szolnok. He had wasted enough time before contacting Count Karpathy in order to show he was alive. She stole a glance at his proud profile. Eyes were fixed ahead as he guided the horses, holding the reins with a lightness of control, the skill of which she recognised, for they were going very swiftly.

'This is exciting,' she remarked.

Valerie hoped he would respond in friendly fashion, but the chill courtesy of his manner disappointed her. He had not forgiven her for asking Kaspar to release him from the absurd promise, and the memory of yesterday's reproaches still hurt. Why were they always quarrelling? She faced the fact that she was half in love with him, maybe on the way to being completely so. Since their first meeting in Magda's house in Vienna she had been gradually drawn towards him and recognised her feeling as totally different from the lukewarm attitude to Kaspar. She found Kaspar dull. He was too committed to the cause of freedom, worthy as it was. This was somewhat remote to Valerie who did not connect the rights of Hungarian peasants with the humiliation heaped upon unfortunate governesses by women like Mrs Pearson. That episode in her life seemed very distant.

Leonin ought to be grateful to her for

prevailing with Kaspar she thought, as the chaise sped along and he maintained his aloofness. With every mile he seemed to look more strongly like the noble heir to Karpathy should look, and she formed an alarming picture of their joint grandfather. It was all very well for Leonin to designate him as oppressive and reactionary, but what was Leonin himself in some respects?

He has been hateful about my darling papa because the Gilliott family sprang from traders, not aristocrats. All right! I am proud of paternal ancestors who made their way in the world instead of merely inheriting wealth and consequence.

And Valerie sat up straight and tilted her chin as she surveyed the passing scene.

They were now on the Alfold plain whose vastness awed her. Grassland stretched as far as her eyes could see, though it was broken now and then by low sandhills, or swamps teeming with birds. Leonin slowed down to skirt one swamp and Valerie heard the weird croaks of what her companion said were cranes. Then he pointed out a heron.

'What a queer bird. Such long legs!'

'Do you know much about birds?'

'Very little,' she confessed.

A mere track, at times obscured, took the place of a proper road. Apart from birds there was a strange emptiness about this section of the Alfold, yet Valerie loved it. She loved the feeling of peace it inspired. She loved the way earth and sky merged into a line of purple on the distant horizon, and the scene, familiar enough to Leonin, caused him to forget his former grievance against this cousin.

He said, 'My nurse used to talk about a cloud of golden towers and turrets that hovered where sky and earth met. Folk of the Alfold really believe such a place exists and call it Fata Morgana's Land. Some swear they have really seen it shining on the horizon.'

'Do you share that belief?'

'It is only a mirage,' he returned.

But the tone of voice expressing disillusionment sounded forced to Valerie's acute ear.

'Who was Fata Morgana?' she asked.

'The Alfold fairy or goddess, who is supposed to exercise a benign influence on those who live here. Men who toil all their lives for a bare existence must have dreams to ease their lot.'

'What is the matter with dreams?'

'My dear cousin, life is meant to be lived, not wasted in foolish imaginings.'

Again Leonin was being irritating, thought Valerie, but with a great effort she kept her temper, concentrating on the enormous expanse and picturing the magic palace of Fata Morgana.

Presently she said aloud, 'Living here would

158

soon convince me that day-dreaming was a pleasurable state, not foolishness. How my mother must have missed the Alfold!'

'Did she say so?'

'No, she never talked about Hungary in any way.'

Not wishing Leonin to vex her with scathing remarks on Lilla having been banished through marriage to a man below her in rank and birth, Valerie turned the conversation quickly to his parents. He declared his mother to be but a vague memory, 'more so than Aunt Lilla.'

'But my father I admired tremendously and I had reached the age of twelve before he was killed by a wild boar. I think he would have made a fine Count Karpathy, although not as enlightened as I shall be. My mother's family was Russian and aristocratic.'

Valerie made no comment. So that he should not notice the pettish look she knew came to her eyes with mention of the word aristocratic, she studied the scene around them. After driving for several more miles they arrived at an isolated dwelling. Leonin called it an inn, but Valerie doubted if there would be any customers but themselves.

'It is used by hunting men and herdsmen, and by the occasional wayfarer like ourselves, but the innkeeper is chiefly concerned with tending his herds of cattle and horses, so leaves the domestic side to his wife. I have spent a night here, but we do not need to do that because we shall reach Karpathy before dark.'

The woman who received them was obliging enough, and the place clean though rather bare. She quickly supplied her guests with a substantial meal of hot sausage, vegetables, potatoes, and savoury pastries that Leonin called turos csusza. There was wine to drink, while a huge water-melon proved even more refreshing.

'You will see plenty of that fruit growing and ripening at Karpathy.'

This was Leonin's only contribution to conversation as they sat down. The woman served them with a respectful humility that embarrassed Valerie because it was so marked, a slave waiting on her master. She expected Leonin to chat to her, not that she, Valerie, would understand since her knowledge of Magyar was still very elementary, although through him and the priest she had learnt a little.

Then she saw her cousin was conveying orders by signs.

'The woman is deaf and dumb,' he explained. 'I gather she expects her husband back soon. He is called Janko and I know he will be able to give me the latest news from Karpathy, including when Tamas Szerb went to Szolnok. Tamas would certainly call here for a meal.'

'Why do this Administrator's movements

160

interest you now?'

'Because I mistrust the man.'

'Is Tamas Szerb the only relation of Aunt Irma?'

'I don't know. The minister, whose daughter our Grandfather deflowered, went to live at Miskolcz, taking the girl, and then Aunt Irma was born there.'

'Yes, you told me Tamas Szerb persuaded Grandfather to take Aunt Irma into the Castle, but he was never very nice to her. I suppose her grandparent, the minister, is dead, but is her mother?'

'I haven't the faintest idea, nor do I care.'

Thus crushed, Valerie applied herself to the meal and the two cousins were silent until the innkeeper, Janko, returned.

He wore a white felt coat with embroidered high collar, and it was unfastened so showed an equally elaborately embroidered waistcoat beneath. Such an outfit would suit Leonin, thought Valerie, for he was looking shabby and the worse for travel. His high boots were covered in dust, his dark breeches had a large tear in them, while his shirt had been badly laundered, and he had no cravat, only an open neck. All the same, Janko bowed low to Leonin and addressed him as Ban, which Valerie already knew to be a title of respect. Even the two white and reddish wolfish dogs at his heels sank on their haunches.

The two men talked rapidly in Magyar. Janko was evidently giving him information which Leonin found displeasing. Valerie had already learnt that when her cousin's brows were drawn together thus meeting in a hard line, it was a sign of vexation.

'What was the man saying?' she asked, as Janko and the dogs moved away.

His wife started to clear the table. Leonin took no notice of either woman, but sat looking fixedly in front of him. Valerie repeated her question.

'My grandfather is seriously ill. Janko was unable to be specific, but it sounds like a stroke, or something of that nature. Slight, I conclude, but severe enough to keep the old man in bed with doctor and nurse, and to have Karpathy village folk saying he won't live long.'

'In that case, why did that horrid libertine, Tamas Szerb, leave him and come to Szolnok? Grandfather might die while he is away.'

'Janko knew the reason for that. He went to meet Aunt Irma and Hugo who were sent for when Grandfather had this stroke.'

'And Aunt Irma, we know, has plans for a false will.'

'It seems I nearly left my homecoming too late,' he admitted gravely.

For the first time during their acquaintance, Valerie could see Leonin was really shaken out of the usual complacency regarding his heritage.

Finding comment impossible, she wisely kept silent. He rose to his feet.

'We'll get on our way without delay.'

She agreed, and soon they were again driving across the plain. She sensed the Alfold had a deeper significance for him than it exerted upon herself, impressed as she was, but the great plain and the village and castle of Karpathy had always been part of Leonin's life. Valerie began to long for the minute when in the distance she should see Karpathy Castle proudly sited on its hill. How often had Leonin proudly proclaimed, 'I am the heir', but just as proudly disregarded her warnings about Aunt Irma's plot to seize Karpathy for herself and her son.

Now the old Count was ill, possibly dying, and the scheming couple had been summoned from Vienna to come immediately. How foolish of Leonin to have wasted precious days in Pest and Szolnok!

'We are nearly there,' he declared in a triumphant tone.

An isolated object, such as Valerie had never seen, stood some distance ahead. The top half had queer attachments that moved with the breeze.

'What is that?'

'A windmill, of course.'

Leonin did not explain its function, only pointed out surrounding fields from which crops of maize would be obtained later in the year. The narrow track widened. Then Valerie saw trees, a huddle of dwellings, and beyond them an isolated hill on which stood a castle. It must be Karpathy Castle that had once been her mother's home.

Without being asked, Leonin confirmed this.

He continued, 'In the centre of those walls, between the battlements, you can see a square tower. That is the principal entrance. It has a portico, only you cannot see that from here.'

'There is another tower on the right, a much shorter one. It looks older. Is it?'

'Yes, it is the relic of an old Turkish fortress that stood there when the Turks were masters of the land.'

'Were they really?'

'Hundreds of years ago. Hungary was one of the first European countries to throw off their yoke. Then this present castle was built.'

He lowered his voice as if fearful of the horses, even the very air, hearing him.

'Just by that ancient tower, and connected with it, is a secret entrance to the Castle. My father showed it to me and he said Grandfather showed it to him, but none of the servants, or rest of the family, knew about it. Creepers grow thick over those old walls and over an iron grille which pulls away to reveal a narrow passage that leads through disused dungeons—so long disused the doors have gone and one can walk up through a series of empty old wine cellars.'

'Oh, take me!' exclaimed Valerie in excitement.

'Maybe, sometime.'

'Aren't you going by that secret entrance?'

'Why should I now? I have no need to go into the Castle by stealth. I shall drive to the proper front portico. But you must wait at the inn until I send word that Grandfather will receive you. Remember he banished your mother for ever, and if he could have caught your father he would have horsewhipped him.'

Valerie turned away her head, wishing to hide her anger from Leonin, but he realised he had gone too far.

'I apologise if I spoke too strongly, Valerie. Perhaps I did speak insultingly.'

'You did,' she returned, astonished that her cousin should at last feel concern about the way he spoke to her.

Leonin actually apologised again. She reminded him the Count replied to her letter of appeal by sending Aunt Irma to England for her, but Leonin again gave voice to his doubts about their grandfather ever receiving her letter.

'Aunt Irma is a wicked woman. Oh, Leonin, don't let her try to get rid of you again.'

'No fear of that,' he laughed. Then he shouted exultantly, 'Karpathy, I come back!'

The village consisted of about thirty thatched cottages, an inn, and a large grey medieval church with a tall steeple. Poplar trees grew at irregular intervals along the narrow single street. They looked as if they had been planted there, not grown by accident, and whatever count had ordered the planting foresaw dignity added to the village's appearance.

The inn where Leonin stopped was a one-storied building, but quite spacious, with a walled courtyard at back and sides. The servant, who came to hold the horses, at once recognised Leonin in spite of the long absence. He hallooed, whereupon another man, obviously the innkeeper, came running out. He stopped short, cried joyfully, 'Ban!' and bowed very low.

They all like Leonin, thought Valerie. His shabby, travel-stained appearance made no difference to the enthusiastic welcome, and she herself felt honoured that the future lord of Karpathy was her first cousin. She knew now that she wanted him to fall in love with her and felt depressed because he showed no sign of doing so. Still, they seemed to have stopped quarrelling, and she was proud to have been made his confidante regarding the Castle's secret entrance.

Was that because he happened to be growing fond of her, or did he intend to smuggle her in that way and confront the old Count with a hitherto unknown granddaughter? For himself he had declared he had no need to go into the

Castle by stealth.

However that might not be the case for her. Her presence was explained to the innkeeper, who made another bow, then led them inside. Valerie gazed approvingly at the large room, as clean as had been Janko's, but better furnished. Instead of tables that were merely scrubbed, these were made of painted beechwood and gleamed with polish. The spring day was quite warm so there was no need for the whitewashed earthenware stove to have been lit. A couple of well-fed looking cats appreciated this, but Valerie was uncomfortably hot.

She noticed the flush on Leonin's cheeks as he listened to the innkeeper, whom he called Gabor, but it was a redness caused by anger not heat of the room. Her knowledge of Magyar was not good enough yet to follow rapid talk. However, Leonin turned round to translate as soon as his conversation with the man was finished.

'Servants at the Castle who have been there for years and personally attended Grandfather —even they are not allowed to go into his bedchamber. When he had the stroke Tamas Szerb naturally assumed complete authority. First he sent a messenger with a letter to Aunt Irma in Vienna.'

'Well that was natural enough. But what about a physician?'

'He went himself to Debrecen for a doctor

167

and two nurses. They are still installed there. Then he went to Miskolcz and brought back an elderly woman. Who do you think she was?'

'How should I know?'

'Old servants recognised her although she had left before she actually bore Aunt Irma.'

'You mean that horrid Tamas Szerb brought Aunt Irma's mother and our grandfather's ex-mistress? Why on earth did he do that?' Was it love, wondered Valerie, then saw the absurdity of her idea. An absence of half a century!

'If Grandfather married the woman, then by law Aunt Irma would become legitimate. You would be relegated to a lower place since your mother was younger than Aunt Irma.'

Valerie gasped in astonishment. Her head was whirling.

'How about you, Leonin?'

'It would not affect me. Male heirs come before females, and as son of Grandfather's only son, of course I am the undisputed heir while I am alive.' He gave an ironical smile. 'Aunt Irma would have learnt from Hugo, after my scrap with him in Vienna, that I escaped death or perpetual imprisonment in Russia, and returned to my own country. I am in no doubt but that she will have made new plans to get me out of the way.'

'Oh, you must be careful. She won't know you are here, but she will as soon as she arrives at Karpathy. Leonin, you must show yourself to Grandfather this very evening.'

'Yes, I am going to the Castle straightaway. I only hope two things.'

'What?'

'That stroke has not made him incapable of recognising people and that Tamas has not already forced through a marriage between him and Adel Vavell.'

'Aunt Irma's mother?'

'Yes, I have just learnt from Gabor that she has been brought from Miskolcz to Karpathy by Tamas Szerb himself.'

'But if Grandfather was unconscious he could not take the vows required for marriage.'

'Any witnesses would be Tamas Szerb's minions. They would swear our Grandfather was conscious and the marriage valid.'

'But the priest who conducted the ceremony?'

'If our local priest—and he is new since I went away—if he refused, then Szerb is quite capable of obtaining a complacent one from Debrecen or Szolnok. It is imperative I go to the Castle and see Grandfather at once.'

The innkeeper was standing listening. Leonin had explained the situation to Valerie in German, so she assumed Gabor did not understand, and it was a surprise to find he had a knowledge of that language as well as his own.

He said in German, 'Ban, servants at the

Castle talk in the village, and we are all distressed by the recent happenings. The doctor brought from Debrecen and the two nurses act completely under Tamas Szerb's orders. So does Adel Vavell. Nobody but those five people is permitted to enter the Count's bedchamber, so he has not been seen by any servants since he collapsed with this stroke. Even his old valet Giskra is kept away.'

'Hasn't the priest been?'

'Oh, I forgot, Ban. When the Administrator brought Adel from Miskolcz, a priest and another man came too, but they have left now. Giskra thinks as you do, that the priest married Adel to the Count. I remember her as a beautiful girl, but so many, many years have passed. She is old, and the Castle servants say she has lost her wits. As for the man who came . . . !'

'Well?' queried Leonin.

'Giskra believes the Count died soon after having the stroke, and the man was an embalmer.'

'You mean that my grandfather is dead, his body has been preserved and remains unburied in his bedchamber?'

'Yes, Ban, that is what is said in the Castle and in the village. Or perhaps I should say, it is whispered. Everyone is too afraid of the Administrator to say so openly.'

'And no funeral will take place until my aunt

arrives. I am supposed to be dead, so she will declare the Count married her mother on his deathbed, thus making her legitimate and able to inherit Karpathy. There is probably a false will drawn up by Tamas Szerb with my grandfather's signature forged on it, and this document will name Aunt Irma as successor.'

The innkeeper solemnly nodded his head.

'I must go to the Castle immediately and establish my rights, which cannot be disputed as I am alive. I know my aunt has tried to persuade my grandfather I am dead. Her lies must be exposed without delay.'

'You need some refreshment first, Ban.'

'I cannot wait. Frau von Moricz may already have reached Szolnok, and been met by Tamas Szerb, and I intend to get into my grandfather's bedchamber before they arrive. No doctors or nurses will keep me out.'

'Nor me,' added Valerie.

Leonin turned towards her.

'You had better wait here, at the inn.'

'No, I am coming with you.'

They had reached what Valerie felt was now a familiar stage, and on this occasion Leonin told her angrily she was to leave him to sort out the matter for himself.

Meanwhile Gabor had fetched glasses and a bottle of wine. He poured out a glass for Leonin who did not refuse it but told the innkeeper to have a horse saddled at once, and was deaf to pleadings to consider a tray of soup, bacon, and groat pottage. Instead he asked if he was right in believing his aunt had spread tales about his death in Russia?

'Giskra said his master refused to believe you had perished.'

'I will show the good Giskra how right he was.'

The servant, who had met Leonin and Valerie in the courtyard and taken charge of the horses hired at Szolnok, now came to announce the Ban's mount was ready. He added what was a vital piece of information.

'Matyas has come from the windmill. A carriage passed him on the road. Seated in it was the Administrator, and with him were Frau von Moricz, and another woman. Herr Hugo was riding behind.'

The other woman would be Magda, thought Valerie, and experienced relief that she and Leonin had one friend in the enemy camp.

CHAPTER TEN

That Karpathy Castle had become a formidable enemy camp was clear enough to Leonin. Valerie saw the effects on his face of a development he had not expected, in spite of her warnings.

'Is that horse saddled yet, Gabor? I want to start at once.' And he added almost to himself, although Valerie heard, 'I was a fool to delay coming home for so long.'

There was more than selfish regret for being outwitted by Aunt Irma in Leonin's voice. He had condemned his grandfather for being a selfish reactionary and a man without affection for others, but Valerie could see Leonin was genuinely concerned about the old Count.

'I refuse to accept this story about death and embalming. I must see for myself. Besides checking Aunt Irma's absurd pretensions, it is high time I confronted her with an accusation of the crime she committed against me. Two years of my life wasted, and I should still be a prisoner in Siberia if I had not had a relative who could secure me a pardon. Two years! I have every justification for seeking vengeance.'

'How are you going to exact it?'

'I don't know yet, but vengeance I shall have.'

Valerie then demanded to accompany him to the Castle. She expected Leonin to demur but they were suddenly interrupted by Gabor. He positively pushed them through a door at the back.

'Ban, you and the lady come this way. I will hide you.'

'Why?'

'It is not safe for you to be seen, Ban. Three

173

police agents and Herr Hugo have ridden into the yard. I saw them coming and made Matyas hide the saddled horse. It will soon be dark, Ban, and then you can get away if they remain here.'

There were loud knockings on the outer door that had been shut and locked when the innkeeper came to warn Leonin. By this time Gabor had pushed the two through a back kitchen and into an outside shed. Here they waited. Valerie knew she was trembling, more from dread of meeting Hugo again than the police officers. But it gave her strength, as well as joy, to feel Leonin's arm round her shoulders. She had taken it for granted he was indifferent to her, that he scorned her because of her mother's so-called misalliance, but this gesture of kindness gave her hope that one day he might feel for her . . . well, what? Love? She knew now she loved him.

'What do you think this means?' she asked, trying to be calm and practical. He must never guess her feelings until he gave tangible proof of his own being as strong as hers, and a very ordinary caress in a critical situation must not be interpreted as more than casual. She added feebly, 'What can Hugo be doing here with police officers? Are they local men?'

'No, Austria and from Vienna.'

'I don't understand.'

'I suspect Aunt Irma has induced Metternich

to send them to deal with me should I show up to claim Karpathy. She must have been scared after learning I had somehow got out of Russia and reached Vienna. Naturally, she would guess my ultimate destination to be Karpathy.'

'But Metternich has fallen from power. He is supposed to have left Austria and he would not come to Hungary. He actually told me he hated the country.'

'He has left behind a weak Emperor and a powerful body of police agents, built up by him and still faithful. They will be plotting for his return and the re-establishment of the Death Room as their interrogation quarters were termed.'

'And do you think Aunt Irma is connected with these secret police agents?'

'For years she has been one of Metternich's amateur spies, very useful and on the outer fringe of his organisation. I am sure she can still call on its aid.'

They were silent for a few minutes, then Leonin exclaimed impatiently that he wished Gabor would come and say what was happening.

'I want to get to the Castle. What a fool I have been to delay matters so long.'

'Cousin Leonin, I intend to come with you to the Castle, and if you say no I shall still follow you. I am not the heir as you are, but I am a grandchild of the man there who is either dead or dying. I was afraid of Hugo just now, but that was silly because he never wanted to marry me, and if his mother has been made legitimate, there will be no need for him to try to make me his wife.'

'Legitimate!' exclaimed Leonin. 'If there has been a marriage to Aunt Irma's mother, my grandfather could not have known what he was doing. In his right senses he would never do such a thing. His notions on rank made that impossible years ago when the woman discovered she was to bear his child. No, I am his heir, only I must show that I am still alive.'

Being alive makes you vulnerable, thought Valerie.

Leonin continued, 'I don't dispute your right to come to the Castle with me. I know I have tried to dissuade you from doing this, but Grandfather has these cast-iron ideas on rank and I was afraid of his humiliating you. It is different now he is very ill and unconscious.'

'Probably dead!'

'So I fear.'

They were silent for a couple of minutes. Then Valerie repeated her opinion that she was no longer of any use to their aunt, but expressed her fears for Leonin's safety. He assured her she need have no anxiety. When he rode up to the Castle all the old servants would know him, while Gabor could spread the news of his return through the village.

'What about the three police agents who have come here with Hugo?'

'How can I know their intention? Certainly I must go into Grandfather's bedchamber and find out if he really is dead. Valerie, I think you had better remain at the inn. I don't want you to run any risk.'

'No, I am coming with you, and that is settled. But is it wise to go openly? You told me about the secret way into the Castle, so why not use that? Once inside, you will be able to find the way to Grandfather's bedroom, won't you?'

'Of course!'

It was quite dark inside the shed now for the sun had set, but Valerie was conscious of her cousin's approval of the suggestion.

He said, 'I shared that secret with you on a sudden impulse and immediately I wondered why I had done so. Then I thought the existence of that passage ought to be known to another member of the family, and who had more right to it than you, Valerie?'

She was glad he could not see her cheeks for she knew she was blushing with pleasure because he had deemed her worthy of such a special confidence. Then the shed door opened. The innkeeper was standing there, holding a lantern.

'Herr Hugo has taken my only two bedchambers, Ban. The one is for those hateful police.' He spat on the ground in contempt.

177

'And your other one?'

'Herr Hugo has booked that for a lady who will be arriving from Szolnok later this evening. She is coming in a hired carriage and stable accommodation must be found for the horses. The driver will have to sleep with his animals, or in my kitchen, but he will only be here for one night.'

'A lady! Did he mention her name?'

'No, Ban.'

'One of Hugo's bits of skirt that he is bringing unknown to his mother.'

Valerie said nothing but inwardly wondered if the 'lady' might be Kataya Strachan, the dismissed maid. Aunt Irma had apparently been ignorant of Kataya's continued presence in Vienna as Hugo's mistress. Extraordinary as it seemed to Valerie, the weak, alcoholic Hugo was quite devoted to Kataya, but this devotion could never exceed a liaison.

If my aunt no longer plans for him to marry me, thought Valerie, then she will surely fix on some girl of Hungarian or Austrian aristocratic family.

The innkeeper said his four guests were being served with a meal, and while they were so occupied Leonin ordered the saddling of a second horse for Valerie, but here came a difficulty. She was only accustomed to riding side-saddle and Gabor's spare horse was not trained to carry a rider in that way.

Eventually Leonin proposed she sat in front of his saddle while he held her to ensure safety.

'We shall keep to a walking pace.'

'Forgive me, Ban, but it does not seem right for the future Count Karpathy to ride in so poor a manner to the Castle, nor is it dignified for the late Countess Lilla's daughter...'

'Don't worry, Gabor. We shall dismount before I knock at the front door to demand entrance.' He whispered to Valerie, 'You know we are not going to any front door.'

She was dazed with excitement. The prospect of at last visiting Karpathy Castle was something she had long pictured, and now she would be riding there on the same horse as Leonin, with his arm holding her. Was more than safety involved? Did he welcome that excuse for close contact? Was he falling in love with her?

He trusts me too, she told herself.

He had told her about the hidden way into the Castle. Triumphantly she recalled his explanation that he made the confidence on momentary impulse, then felt it was her right to share the important secret. He felt 'the existence of that passage ought to be known to another member of the family.'

Then another aspect of the situation came into Valerie's mind and made her tremble. He would be in danger from Aunt Irma's plots once his return was known, and she dreaded what the unscrupulous creature, aided by Hugo, might do. There were those police agents whom Irma must have obtained to help her claim the title and estate from an old man either dead or dying. Valerie was filled with regret that Leonin had not contacted their grandfather before this disastrous stroke.

She was hurried up a steep back staircase by a woman who was evidently Gabor's wife and under orders to permit only a few minutes for a face wash and hair combing. Valerie's gown was suitable for travelling by carriage but hardly for riding a horse, and she gathered from the woman that her baggage had been hidden in an out house, well away from prying eyes. The only extra left was a dark cloak which would certainly be useful.

Escorted outside again, the dim lantern light revealed that Leonin did not look the same untidy traveller. His coat had been brushed, his boots polished, and round his neck he wore a silk cravat. Gabor had been determined the Ban should bear some signs of the role he must represent as Count, or heir to the Count.

The horse set out, pacing slowly in the darkness. Soon Leonin guided it off the main road, and Valerie guessed they were on the Castle front drive, but that was not for long. There came a turn to the right, then one to the left. By now they were passing through a dense wood, but gradually the growth of trees became

180

thinner and it was possible to see, in the now bright moonlight, a ghostly outline of turrets and battlements ahead. So this was Karpathy Castle! It might have been the mystical abode of Fata Morgana, but as the horse climbed upwards Valerie found it looked vividly real and substantial.

Near the high solid outer wall of the Castle, Leonin checked the horse, dismounted, and lifted Valerie down, her boots and hem of gown becoming hidden in the long grass, though she managed to pull her cloak in time. Trees were few and stunted, but short bushes grew everywhere as well as grass, and the lower part of the encircling grey stone wall was partly obscured by creepers, and the tendrils of these creepers created a mysterious tangle that looked all the more exciting with moonlight shining upon the wall and the ground below.

'Surely all the Castle is not like this,' remarked Valerie. 'It seems deserted here—no servants, no people . . .'

'Do you see that old tower to the right, just within the wall?'

'Yes, that is the Turkish tower you pointed out to me before we reached Karpathy village.'

'Folk from the village and folk from the Castle avoid the Turkish tower, and of course the wall surrounding it, though that was built later. There is a story of a Turkish ruler and tyrant being murdered here, and his ghost is supposed to haunt the spot. Not that I ever believed such a yarn, but then I am not superstitious, nor was my father.'

'Is Grandfather?'

'I have no idea about him,' said Leonin. 'But the spot is deserted and of no interest. I don't know why I was attracted to it, but that was how I found the secret way in and out of the Castle. Now I must look for it, and that may not be easy after not using it for years. Somewhere behind the mass of creeper, and where the wall passes the tower, an iron grille hides the narrow hole giving access.'

He tethered the horse, took Valerie's hand to assist her over the rough ground, then released her as he began to search through dense creeper for the entrance.

'I used to know exactly where it was, but I seem to have forgotten now.'

'You'll soon remember,' was Valerie's encouraging remark, though she herself was fearful he might not.

Perhaps it would be better to go boldly to the principal front entrance of the Castle and demand admittance to the old Count's bedchamber. According to Gabor's tale, only doctor, nurses, Tamas Szerb, and Aunt Irma's mother were allowed inside that room. Soon, in addition there would be Aunt Irma, and later Hugo. Valerie thought of Hugo supping with the police agents as he waited for Kataya Strachan.

She waited while Leonin's hands explored the wall which was so hidden by creeper. Entrance, such as it was, must be low down, for he stooped as he followed a line quite near the ground, but at last he gave a subdued cry of triumph and began to tear at the growth, throwing ends to wither among grass and shrubs. The moon had vanished behind a cloud so he lit the small lantern he had been carrying and held it against a portion of the wall close to the Turkish tower. Valerie saw an iron grille.

'That is it!'

The grille was loose and easily removed to reveal a narrow opening into which Leonin crawled and then extended a hand for his companion.

Valerie saw they were in a narrow cavern but high enough for them to stand upright, and at the end came a flight of stone steps. She could not see how high they were or what lay beyond. Holding Leonin's hand she began to ascend, thankful she was not alone and that he had a light. She hated the heavy damp smell that had met them when coming into the cavern, but it grew less as they climbed upwards reaching what was clearly meant for a wine cellar. It had two exits.

Leonin pointed to the one on the right.

'That leads to the Turkish tower, but we shall take the other way and after a couple more cellars get to one that has access to the Castle proper,' he explained.

What Leonin called the final cellar was stored with bottles of wine, but, judging by the cobwebs, many must have lain maturing there for some time. There were a few more steps. At the top had once been a door, but that was no longer visible, only an opening to a long bare passage. At one point, a shut door and the sound of voices indicated humans, possibly domestics. Leonin tip-toed past that door, then turned to help Valerie up a winding staircase, evidently used by the servants.

Now they were in a lighted corridor, resplendent with marble pillars, mahogany furniture, and thick carpet. A second flight led to a passage equally grand. Valerie noticed the doors were painted white and had golden knobs. Without hesitation, Leonin stopped in front of one, turned the knob, opening it, and stepped inside, gently drawing Valerie after him.

The only light in the room was that shed by his lantern. Vaguely Valerie noted the red damask walls and buff-coloured draperies, but her attention was concentrated on the huge canopy bed with crimson silk hangings. Leonin left her and walked towards it, looking intently at the figure lying there. He bent over it, but Valerie guessed the answer when she approached and her cousin turned to face her.

'Grandfather is dead.'

He knelt down and gazed reverently at the corpse. All his life he had defied this grandparent who never showed affection, only dominated those who came in contact with him. In his way, the Count did care for his son and his son's son, but neither perceived this.

Julius Karpathy had a strong element of laziness in his make-up. He conformed because that was easier and more comfortable than opposition. One day, he told himself, he would become Count Karpathy, and then he should permit that admirable son of his to have his way over bettering the peasants and other tenants. The same indolence made him neglect his Russian-born wife, from whom Leonin evidently inherited his extraordinary energy. Indolence was also the cause of Julius's lack of sympathy with his sister Lilla, who behaved so foolishly over that Englishman and in the end ran away with him. As for Irma, Julius considered his father spoke cruelly about her illegitimate birth, for the girl could not help it, but he himself disliked this bastard half-sister. He knew she had a cunning nature. The sight of her dead grandfather had an hypnotic effect upon Valerie. She did not kneel by the bedside like Leonin. She just stood as if memorising the noble features of the relative, seen at last, and who for so long had been a mystery to her.

Desperation had made her write to him for

financial assistance. Then Aunt Irma appeared on the scene, apparently sent by him to take her to Karpathy Castle. Valerie now blamed her own credulity for believing everything said by her aunt, but she pictured an old man, anger softened by time and wanting to show kindness to Lilla's child. That conception of the situation wavered as she became aware of Aunt Irma's true nature.

Did he even know Mama had a daughter? Valerie asked herself as she gazed at the lifeless, embalmed object, that had once been Count Karpathy.

'He is dead,' repeated Leonin.

'But he ought to be buried, not left like this.'

'A cunning arrangement made by Tamas Szerb in my aunt's absence. Grandfather will die officially after her arrival, so she will take charge of the obsequies because she will claim the estate. I can see her flourishing the false certificate of marriage between Grandfather and her mother, Adel Vavell.'

'Do you believe there has been such a marriage?'

'I believe in a false ceremony.'

'But you are the proper legal heir, Leonin. In fact you are now the Count.'

'And, thank God, I have got here in time to prove it. If I had delayed longer to help Kaspar, she might have cooked up something to deprive me of my rights, as she thought she had done while I was in Russia. I expect she has obtained the services of those Viennese police agents to prevent me from approaching the Castle and claiming my own.'

'You have stolen a march on her then. I am so glad.'

'Are you prepared to come into the open with me, Valerie, and face her? I shall see she does not harm you.'

'Of course I will. I hate Aunt Irma and her lies. I loathe Hugo too. What are you going to do next?'

'Show myself, say I have ascertained my grandfather is dead so I am now the Count, and the only person entitled to arrange the funeral ... Gracious, who is this?'

For the bedchamber door had opened to admit a little wizened woman, like a far older edition of Aunt Irma but small in stature and without Irma's elegance. She gave a horrified scream at seeing Leonin and Valerie.

'He is mine,' she cried piteously like a child whose favourite toy is to be taken away. 'He did marry me at last. Yes, I am a lawfully married woman and my daughter Irma is legitimate. She will now inherit Karpathy, and my grandson Hugo from her. Hugo will become Irma's heir.'

It was like a lesson learnt by rote, thought Valerie. Adel Vavell, poor thing, was quite senile. Leonin ignored her. Again he seized Valerie's hand and steered her towards the doorway and into the corridor, but they had only walked a short distance when another woman appeared. It was a woman both were pleased to see.

'Magda!' exclaimed Valerie, embracing her.

She was frightened of this Castle, feeling Leonin's present position was fraught with danger, so the appearance of a sensible and trustworthy ally was very reassuring. She watched Leonin greet Kaspar's mother with the respect he might have accorded to a lady of noble birth, which Magda was not, though not the abigail she pretended to be. Was he modifying the foolish notions drawn from their grandfather? Valerie had never been able to see how they fitted with the ideals expounded by Kossuth, and to which he and Kaspar were pledged to conform.

'I suppose you arrived from Szolnok with my aunt earlier this evening,' Leonin was saying. 'Did you know my grandfather was dead? I am Count Karpathy now.'

'Yes, Count. The Administrator sent a messenger with the news to Buda.'

Buda was the Hungarian town on the opposite side of the Danube to Pest, but unlike Pest it was strongly pro-Austrian, thus an obvious refuge for the von Moricz mother and son if Vienna was uncomfortable. According to Magda the capital was still in a state of unrest, and though some feared the weak emperor might recall Metternich, nobody believed this, certainly not Frau von Moricz.

'Metternich favourites, and of course his spies, were too nervous to stay,' continued Magda. 'They decided to leave Vienna and stay in Buda until they saw what happened, but on receipt of the Administrator's letter—and I managed to read it—they set out for Szolnok to meet that objectionable Tamas Szerb.'

Valerie agreed silently that he was objectionable, but surely he did not take liberties with Magda? He might, despite her age and lack of attraction.

'Does Frau von Moricz know you are here, Count?'

'She does not, nor Tamas Szerb, nor my cousin Hugo, but they soon will. I was just about to proclaim myself and assume authority for my late grandfather's funeral.'

Leonin was conducting both women further along the corridor and at the far end he opened a door, flashing his lantern, then lighting a lamp inside the room. Valerie noticed the faded carpet and draperies, and how such a large room only contained a bed, desk, and a few chairs. She got the impression it had not been used for a long time, so much of its original contents had been removed while those left bore obvious signs of neglect.

'This was my bedchamber from boyhood until I left to study at Vienna University. More than five years since I stepped inside! Anyway, we can talk in peace. I suppose you are anxious for the latest news of Kaspar, Frau Webber. I left him in Szolnok, where you too have been, but he plans to go to Debrecen in a week and I have promised to contact him there. I have to convey to him a substantial donation that will be of great help in recruiting volunteers to fight for Kossuth when need arises.'

'So he will still be at Szolnok. If only I had known where he was staying before I left the place.'

'I can give you that information. I take it you are planning to quit my aunt's service then?'

'There is no point in remaining, since her spying activities have ended with Prince Metternich's downfall, and I am certain he will never return to power in Austria. Like Hungary, she is set on a fight for freedom, and people like Frau von Moricz know that. I heard her say so to your Administrator. But, Count, are you aware that she means to claim this estate and title? I gather a marriage was conducted between your grandfather, when unconscious and possible already dead, and a woman fetched from Miskolcz who is the Frau's mother?'

'I know all about that,' said Leonin. 'And I hope to prove the marriage a fraud, but even if I cannot yet I am Count through being the only son of my late grandfather's son. Aunt Irma realises I got away from Russia, but she is not aware I am at Karpathy. I have seen the corpse and know death took place some days ago. The body was embalmed.'

'Do be careful of yourself, Sir,' urged Magda. 'Frau von Moricz will try again to get rid of you because you stand between her and the fulfilment of her ambitions.'

'The servants in the Castle and the villagers and farmers will all stand loyally by me,' said Leonin confidently. 'I am going to show myself in the servants' hall before I face my aunt. She will not dare to dispute my position.'

'Do you wish me to remain here? I will do so if I can be of assistance. What are Kaspar's plans?'

'He will be starting for Debrecen in a week. No, thank you, Frau, you must go to him. In fact, by doing so, you can perform me a service. As I said, I intended to go to Debrecen and join him there, but the situation here makes that difficult. I have to arrange my grandfather's funeral with all the pomp and ceremony that befits a Hungarian nobleman. It is a duty I must perform and will take several days.'

Leonin then turned questioningly to Valerie, but she burst out with determination that he could not send her away.

'As a grandchild, I insist on taking my rightful place among the mourners, and that means I have precedence before Aunt Irma and Hugo.'

He accepted her claim. The days of opposition seemed to have ended thought Valerie. She listened to him explaining to Magda how she could serve him.

'I take it you want to return to Szolnok, and by hiring a conveyance you can get there before Kaspar leaves.'

'Do you think I can obtain one in Karpathy village?'

'I am sure of that. One is due from Szolnok this evening bringing a so-called lady friend of my Cousin Hugo, and leaving her at the inn. Talk to the innkeeper and he will arrange for it to take you to your son tomorrow. This is where Kaspar is staying.'

And he wrote the address of the priest who had given the three hospitality.

Magda took the slip of paper and thanked him, but she wanted to know what practical help she could give.

'You said that by going to my son I could be of use to you as well.'

'I will explain,' and he went to the desk standing at one end of the room. 'Come here—both of you!'

The two women watched him moving fingers cautiously over its surface until at last those fingers touched a concealed spring which moved part of the desk's very thick lid and revealed a cavity large enough to show a velvet bag. Leonin drew this out and closed the aperture.

192

'This contains my mother's jewellery and I promised Kaspar he should have it to sell for the cause.'

Valerie had expected larger pieces and more of them, but the brilliance of those placed by Leonin on a table proclaimed their value. There were several pearl necklaces, some a single string, some two or three. There was a beautiful emerald and diamond necklace that she would have loved to put round her own neck, and an exquisite emerald bracelet, then on a chain a pear shaped emerald pendant. Leonin drew her attention to a necklace of rubies that he called 'pigeon's blood.' Turquoises, sapphires, amethysts—Valerie gazed at the collection with awe.

'You are really intending to present these to the Kossuth cause!' she exclaimed.

'There are family jewels stored—well! somewhere in the Castle, and they are always worn by the Count's wife, but these are a private set, kept by my father. He placed them here in my keeping when my mother died and though I was a mere boy he said I was the only person who knew she had these gems. There had been no formal entertaining at the Castle for years, nor did she and my father go to seek social life in Buda or Vienna, so she had had no opportunity of wearing them. I think any woman I marry would understand why I wish to offer them for sale to raise funds for Hungary

193

to become free from the Austrian yoke, and for Austria herself to gain liberty.'

Leonin turned to Magda.

'Rather than wait until I can spare time to hand these jewels personally to Kaspar at Debrecen, will you, Frau Webber, convey them to him when you meet at Szolnok tomorrow night?'

'Willingly, Count,' promised Magda. Then she became practical. 'I do not quite know how I can leave the Castle without being seen, yet I must get to the village inn you spoke about.'

'There is a secret way, and I shall escort you to the inn myself. Valerie, come with us to the outer wine cellar and wait for my return, because you must not be seen by Aunt Irma until we can appear together.'

So Magda was to be the third person entrusted with the hidden way into Karpathy Castle.

CHAPTER ELEVEN

'Isn't there anywhere else I can wait?' asked Valerie as they passed through the successive wine cellars and began to descend the steps leading to the entrance grille.

It would be foolish of her to ask Leonin if she could accompany him and Magda further, for she knew she would be a drag on them during the walk to the village. She was already tired by the long day's exertions, and there was only the one horse available and he had not been trained for a lady's mount.

'I know it is a dreary place,' replied Leonin. 'But here you will not be found, and I promise to be as quick as I can. I must ensure everything is in order for Frau Webber to go to Szolnok tomorrow, and then we shall both present ourselves to Aunt Irma. Don't worry! I am master here and I will protect you. By now she will know you are here.'

'You mean that queer mother of hers will have spread the news that there were strangers in Grandfather's bedroom, and she will have guessed who those strangers were. That is if Aunt Irma believes the poor woman, but she did not seem to be in full possession of her wits.'

'Adel Vavell is afflicted with one of the disabilities of old age, and in her case her mind has failed more than her years warrant. But Aunt Irma will take her chatter seriously now. I expect she has already started a search of the Castle, but she will never think of your being hidden down here. She is unlikely ever to have been in these cellars, and the old Turkish tower is a place avoided by all except my father and me. I can assure you no ghost walks there, Valerie. Tales get about, and peasants and servants are very credulous.'

'I am not afraid,' declared Valerie proudly. 'It is just that the place is dismal. Can I have your lantern?'

'Of course. It will be moonlight outside. Now I promise I will be as quick as I can. I am anxious to claim my rights as Count Karpathy.'

'I daresay I can find my own way to the village, My Lord.'

Leonin shook his head.

'No, Frau Webber, I want to see the innkeeper personally and explain the situation to him, also advise about spreading news of my return throughout the village.'

'But those police agents! Oh, Leonin, do be careful of them. They might try to arrest you.'

'They cannot do that, Valerie.'

Leonin put his hand in the pocket of his breeches, and Valerie noticed how Gabor had seen that the tear was neatly mended. Leonin drew out a document clipped to two passports—one genuine and the other a false one which presumably he showed when crossing from Austria into Hungary with Kaspar.

'This official pardon in Russian and German guarantees safety from arrest by any police, including Metternich's men whose attendance here must have been requested by Aunt Irma.'

'Prince Metternich has fled abroad,' put in Magda. 'Frau von Moricz is not useful to those

196

who have succeeded him, and that is why I am anxious to leave her and rejoin my son. It is a waste of time for me to remain as abigail when I could be near Kaspar and help him.'

'You must have hated serving my aunt.'

'Indeed I did, Fraulein Valerie.'

'I'll see you safely in the charge of my good friend the innkeeper,' said Leonin. 'He will provide you with transport to Szolnok, and if my Cousin Hugo is still at the village inn, Gabor will keep you out of his sight. Do you know who is this lady friend that Hugo is waiting for?'

'The abigail Frau von Moricz employed before me—oh, for a year or so because Madam brought her to Karpathy on her last visit, but dismissed her because Herr Hugo was too impressed by her bright eyes. She is German and was supposed to go back to that country, but I know, and so does Fraulein Valerie, that he was secretly keeping her in Vienna.'

'I am aware my Cousin Hugo has a flirtatious side,' was Leonin's sarcastic understatement. 'And so you followed this favourite, Frau Webber?'

'Her name is Kataya Strachan. Yes, the rumour reached my son's organisation that the Metternich spy, Frau von Moricz, was requiring a new personal maid, and one not endowed with youth and beauty who would attract Herr Hugo.' She shrugged her

197

shoulders.

Magda certainly lacked youth when she could be the mother of a son who was about thirty. Though not good-looking, she was not ugly, and Valerie thought Leonin ought to have had the courtesy to introduce a compliment, but this was hardly the occasion for social intercourse. They walked from the last cellar and down the steps leading to the entrance closed by the grille. Valerie agreed to sit on the bottom step while she waited for Leonin's return. He had somehow collected a skin rug and, with Magda's help, this was spread out for her.

Heartened by his assurances that he would not be long away and by Magda's obvious concern, Valerie assumed a nonchalance she certainly did not feel. She hated the dank smell of the place. She hated doing nothing while Leonin was actively engaged in forwarding his plans. That is, if you could call his fulfilling the promise of donating those jewels, necessary to his determination to claim the Karpathy title and estate, but that was absurd.

He has wasted too much time helping Kaspar and the Kossuth cause, was Valerie's opinion.

Oh, God, grant he comes back quickly.

She must occupy her thoughts constructively, but no constructive role stretched in front of her, only passive waiting for Leonin to return and act. For the first time, Valerie realised that while sheer necessity had driven her to approach her grandfather, his death now meant nothing to her, while she longed to become part of this strange land, amid surroundings that had once been her mother's. But it was not her mother's influence. Lilla had scarcely spoken of Hungary. Leonin was the one who personified that country for Valerie. He loved it, and she loved him. Neither wealth nor position came into that love, though she knew she would welcome being the mistress of Karpathy because through that she could help him to achieve the reforms he believed in.

Yes, he did believe in the spirit of the Kossuth cry of Liberty, Equality, Fraternity. She remembered that fateful March day in Vienna when they were taking a roundabout route to reach Kaspar's home unseen, and how Leonin talked then about his convict days in Siberia and how people in Russia were oppressed worse than those in Austria or Hungary. With great sincerity he had said proudly he would behave differently from his grandfather towards peasants when he became Count Karpathy. Now he was master of those lands.

But would belief in Equality be strong enough to sweep away the inherited snobbery concerning blood of nobility? Again and again he had angered Valerie with contemptuous remarks about her father's non-aristocratic lineage, but not recently. Valerie remembered that his treatment of her became different as they began to ride across the Alfold plain. Was it the magic influence of Fata Morgana? On leaving Szolnok he was sulky because she had persuaded Kaspar that it was important Leonin presented himself at Karpathy Castle without further delay. Her heart glowed as she remembered Leonin's acknowledgement of his foolishness in delaying his homecoming so long.

Valerie shivered and pulled the animal skin on which she was sitting closer, so that it would keep the draughts from her. A draughty, dank-smelling, grim place, she thought miserably. The lantern light showed the end of the narrow cavern, and as she was on the bottom step of the flight leading to wine cellars, the iron grille was just visible. How she longed for the moment when that grille would be pulled aside from without, and Leonin re-appear!

Now she began to worry about his safety. Gabor, the innkeeper, was obviously trust-worthy, but if the police agents became awkward would he be able to allay their suspicions? Supposing they searched the inn. Supposing they encountered Leonin arriving with Magda, and then Hugo denounced his cousin. Would the Tsar's pardon save Leonin? He said it would, although he had kept himself hidden in Vienna. Valerie now was at a stage when fear for his safety overwhelmed her.

It required a frantic effort of willpower to remain seated on the step and fix her gaze intently on the grille, longing for it to be pulled aside and for her beloved to scramble through. At last she became weary of watching. She shut her eyes and pictured his face—the straight nose, high cheek bones, proud lips, and fair hair. His eyes were of the same shade of grey as her own. She knew that, on recalling a conversation overheard on her first evening in Vienna. Hugo was being told by Aunt Irma that his cousin had 'the Karpathy grey eyes,' and Leonin was supposed to be a typical Karpathy. Valerie also remembered Hugo asking his mother sardonically about 'my maternal grandmother's colouring', taunting Aunt Irma with her bastard birth.

I did not know then that Aunt Irma was born out of wedlock, Valerie said to herself, and she had to admit that Aunt Irma probably suffered a good deal through the illegitimacy which was not her fault. Did not Leonin say their grandfather used to remind her of it? No wonder she was so ambitious for herself and Hugo. Her nature had possibly been warped by continual snubbings.

At last Valerie's musings were interrupted by the slight sound of the grille being pulled away. She opened her eyes and there was Leonin scrambling through the aperture. Her relief was so great she forgot all about dignity and rushed towards him. He straightened his tall frame after the bending, and held out his arms towards her. Encircled by those arms and radiant with joy that he had returned safely, she pressed against him, conscious of being treasured, conscious of being truly loved.

Passionate kisses were recklessly given, his lips on hers and she returning them. Reluctantly he released her, and very slowly. Valerie thought how different were Leonin's kisses from the hateful ones once inflicted upon her by Hugo. Those she feared as she did possible ones from Tamas Szerb which she was thankful to escape. But here was the man she loved. Leonin was the hero she felt she had sought all her life, and he was real, not the insubstantial phantom of a Fata Morgana day-dream.

He was apologising for being away so long and praising her patience. Valerie, with a tinge of amusement, longed to confess she had been terrified in this miserable place, and had only remained because she had no alternative. He was compelled to wait longer at the inn than he intended, hidden of course. Kataya Strachan arrived in a smart carriage Hugo had hired for her in Szolnok, and her driver also brought written instructions from the police chief in that town, relaying a message from Vienna. There had been a second rising in the Austrian capital.

This was against the Emperor Ferdinand who, weak and irresolute, had broken his promises and was rumoured to be trying to recall Prince Metternich. The three police agents sent to assist Frau von Moricz in establishing her claim to Karpathy, were summoned to Vienna, so immediately set off on horseback to Szolnok where a train would be available. They were obliged to hire, or rather commandeer, village horses since the swifter animals which had brought Kataya required a night's rest, as did those which had originally brought them.

'Gabor concealed me until both police and Hugo had left. Hugo set out for the Castle and will be with Aunt Irma now.'

'Does she know Kataya is in Karpathy?'

'Of course not. Hugo keeps quiet about his amusements. He is only having a liaison with the girl, and it cannot be anything more, but our aunt watches lest he commits any unintentional indiscretion. You must have realised, Valerie, how badly he drinks.'

'Adel Vavell saw us in Grandfather's bedchamber, so she will have told Aunt Irma and Hugo. She would not know who I was but she would recognise you, wouldn't she?'

'I doubt it. She has never seen me before because she was settled at Miskolcz before I was born. Anyway, darling, let us show ourselves. I want the entire Castle to know the new Count Karpathy is here and in charge. Meanwhile, late as the hour is, Gabor is spreading the news throughout the village.'

'Hugo will hear it and tell Aunt Irma.'

'Unless I show myself first. Darling, she will not dare to put up any opposition.'

'What about her past schemes, like your death and the marriage you believe to be false?'

'It was false, for Grandfather would never have taken part in such a ceremony. I suspect the idea came from Tamas Szerb. A legitimate-born Irma with the true heir imprisoned in Siberia could ensure inheritance of Karpathy, but our aunt and Szerb know it is useless when I turn up alive.'

'Yes,' agreed Valerie. 'But having failed this time to get you out of the way, I am dreadfully afraid of another attempt on you. Leonin, you must be constantly on your guard against their treachery. You will, won't you?'

'Don't worry,' he said, and then turned to another subject. 'While I was enduring the misery of being a convict in Siberia, I swore revenge on Aunt Irma. I vowed that if I managed to regain my freedom I should make her suffer as I was doing. I thought about it in Vienna, and on the journey through Hungary and across the Alfold, but now I am back in Karpathy, revenge seems unimportant.'

'What will you do?'

'Probably nothing.'

'Oh, Leonin, surely you won't permit her to

live peacefully at this family Castle?'

'Heavens, no! As soon as Grandfather's remains have been suitably interred, she and Hugo and Adel Vavell, and Tamas Szerb leave my lands for ever. I shall not do anything but banish them because I no longer want revenge, but I could not endure their presence. They can go to Miskolcz or Vienna.'

'You are very forgiving.'

Even in the dim light of a lantern she could see the happy smile that lit up his face.

'Who would not be forgiving when he had the love of a wonderful girl like you! By the way, I have not asked you if you will marry me.'

'Are you doing so now?'

'Doesn't it sound like an offer? Excuse my clumsiness but I have never done this before.'

'And you don't mind my father having come of merchant stock?'

'Valerie, forgive me for the abominable things I have said. They were a hang-over from notions instilled into me as a child, and of which I now am ashamed. I ought not to blame my dead grandfather but he was a hardened old tyrant and obsessed with feudal ideas. Many of them my father rejected, but Papa had married a member of the Russian aristocracy, and again I came under traditional notions that now I realise are absurd. I disagreed with him and Grandfather over treatment of our peasants, so I was ready to absorb what Kaspar taught me. He and I became friends at Vienna University. Then I stayed with relatives in Russia and the time spent on their country estates horrified me. The poor devils there had a far worse time than any of our Hungarian vassals, although things are bad enough here and I shall alter them. You will help me, won't you, darling?'

'Of course I will. But I am very worried about what Aunt Irma might do to you. She has made one nearly disastrous attempt against your life, and with a second . . . '

'She dare not try now,' declared Leonin confidently.

'I am not so sure. Anyway, you must be careful. Oh, it is noble of you to put aside all thought of revenge, but that will not alter her evil intentions.'

He laughed lightly.

'Nothing is noble when I am the fortunate possessor of you and Karpathy.'

His voice changed to a more serious note.

'I have always hated our aunt and Tamas Szerb, but I do realise now that she was abominably treated by Grandfather. He brought her from Miskolcz as a young girl to be nothing but a menial in this household, and I can remember him taunting her about her birth. It was all wrong.'

Valerie could see how such a humiliating upbringing contradicted the beliefs acquired by

Leonin through his association with Kaspar. He meant to be a model nobleman. She swore to be a wife who would help him to carry out his aspirations.

That task would not be easy. However magnanimously Leonin treated Aunt Irma, Hugo, and Tamas Szerb, she was under no delusion that they were unpleasant characters, possibly made so by the circumstances of their lives, but unscrupulous enemies. They would take his clemency as weakness.

Valerie and Leonin had emerged from the wine cellars to walk along a stone corridor lined with doors. 'Store cupboards,' said Leonin. Then he opened a wider door which gave access to a large kitchen where four maidservants were engaged in fetching dishes from an adjoining room and taking in fresh ones. They were the lower rank of servants waiting on their superiors, who sat in the Servants' Dining Hall. Valerie did not know this. She sniffed hungrily at the smell of soup coming from a simmering cauldron hanging from a hook over a fire. Leonin strode ahead, ignoring the astonished looks of the menials busy in their task, and Valerie found herself ushered into the adjoining room.

With one accord all rose to their feet as they recognised their new master, although he had been absent for a few years.

An elderly man, small of stature and with a

thin wrinkled face, came forward, assuming the right of seniority and importance which permitted him to greet Leonin.

He said gravely, though relief and real pleasure were mingled in the greeting, 'Welcome back to Karpathy, My Lord Count.'

'Giskra!' exclaimed Leonin. 'Yes, I know that my grandfather is dead and only his embalmed corpse lies in the bedchamber upstairs. One of my first duties will be to arrange for his proper funeral.'

Giskra nodded his head gravely and Valerie sensed that the remainder of these higher servants, mostly elderly, approved.

'None of us has been permitted to go near the Count—the late Count—since he suffered that stroke. Even I who have been his valet for forty years, I have been forcibly excluded by that abominable Tamas Szerb. As Administrator he claimed to be acting on the orders of Frau von Moricz, but she has only arrived today. According to Tamas Szerb, a priest from Miskolcz married the Count to Adel Vavell since his illness, and Frau von Moricz claims to have been rendered legitimate. You have been reported dead, My Lord, and Frau Irma succeeds you as owner of Karpathy.'

'You can all see I am not dead. And I do not believe this supposed marriage to be authentic, Giskra. Not that it alters the situation, since legitimate or illegitimate, I am Count. Frau von

Moricz never had any claim.'

Leonin suddenly became conscious of Valerie standing beside him.

'This is the lady who is my heir until I marry and have lawful children. She is the daughter of my late Aunt Lilla and she comes before distant cousins and certainly Frau von Moricz.'

It was flattering to receive respectful obeisances from servants who had known her mother. Moreover Valerie felt pride in belonging to the noble family of Karpathy as she graciously acknowledged the tributes. Leonin took them for granted. She listened to him telling Giskra, and therefore the rest of the company, how he had penetrated his grandfather's bedchamber and seen the embalmed corpse. He did not explain how he got into the Castle unseen, nor that the only witness of his and Valerie's discovery was Adel Vavell. The last-named had rushed about screaming there were intruders.

'Tamas Szerb gave orders for a search to be made of the Castle, but Adel's cries were so incoherent, and it is known her wits have gone, so the alarm was not taken seriously. She is a sad old woman now, whereas once she was respected as a minister's daughter and, for a brief period, reigned as the Count's favourite. I had not seen her for nearly fifty years, Ban, and I would not have recognised her.'

In reply to further questioning by Leonin,

Giskra stated that Hugo von Moricz had only arrived half an hour ago, and was now in the salon with his mother, his despised grandmother, and the shifty powerful relative, Tamas Szerb.

'Very well, I shall now escort my cousin to the salon and we will both confront my aunt. I have urgent orders to give since as Count Karpathy it is my duty to arrange for the funeral of the late Count. I also have to announce my betrothal to Miss Gilliott, my cousin.'

Leonin looked a little apprehensively at Valerie as if afraid he had been presumptuous, but her happy, confiding smile reassured him, and together they acknowledged cheers and congratulations. Then, accompanied by Giskra, who obviously assumed that his was the privilege of announcing them to the woman and two men he hated, they left the domestic quarters, ascended another flight of stairs, and reached the principal part of the Castle.

And this was impressive, as Valerie had felt before when she passed along corridors brilliant with lights from candelabra, but then her mind was too occupied to absorb the beauty and grandeur as it did now. Nor had she been very far before they reached her grandfather's bedchamber.

Now she and Leonin followed Giskra along a gallery that overlooked an enormous hall.

Leading to it were two sets of stairs with wide shallow marble steps. They descended by one side and she gazed at the massive hall, yes massive but crowded with suits of armour and, adorning the walls, stuffed heads of boars and wolves. Dark wooden panelling was given light by candelabra, malachite pillars, and a vivid crimson carpet.

Giskra flung open a pair of double doors. Valerie was almost amused by the grandeur of his voice as he loudly announced the heir whom he loved and whose life had been in doubt for so long.

'The Count of Karpathy and Miss Gilliott.'

My name does sound feeble beside Leonin's title, thought Valerie. Then her attention was claimed by the reaction on the four people in the room. Aunt Irma looked overcome with rage, her mother shrieked that these wicked intruders had been in the bedchamber just as she said, Tamas Szerb's face was impassive, but it was on Hugo that Valerie's attention was fixed.

She had always held him in contempt. Before they actually met, disillusionment came in the conversation between him and Aunt Irma that she overheard in the Vienna house salon. However at the first meeting she was forced to admit he was extremely good-looking and gave the impression of intense vitality, but now his tendency to excessive drinking was obvious. His eyes and cheeks were puffy and even his clear-cut features coarsened, while he seemed to have lost previous interest in his mother's claim to Karpathy, a claim really directed towards his own benefit. Valerie felt he no longer cared about being in line for title and ownership. Possibly he had realised, when he saw Leonin alive and in Vienna the day of the rising that Irma's plans were hopeless.

For the first time it occurred to Valerie that possibly Hugo had no ambition to become Count Karpathy. He preferred the slipshod, drunken, somewhat immoral existence he led in Vienna, only to continue thus he needed money and she wondered if his lucrative post would be safe now Metternich had been exiled.

Certainly there was no question about Aunt Irma's ambition remaining unchanged, nor of the Administrator's support. Tonight they stood facing Leonin, looking secure and dominating, while the elderly Adel Vavell twittered nervously like a frightened hen until given a sharp reproof by her daughter. This so terrified the poor creature that her mouth closed in the middle of a sentence and she crept to a large sofa, clinging to its back as if attempting to hide.

'Your scheme to have me permanently banished to Siberia failed.'

Leonin's voice rang out, accusing and full of anger.

212

'I do not know what you are talking about.'

'You do, so lies are useless. Understand that once Grandfather has been buried I never want to set eyes upon you or your associates again. I include Hugo and Tamas Szerb. You will leave Karpathy for good, the village, the lands as well as the Castle.'

'Not so quickly, nephew! You are not master here, so have no power to order me or my son out of our rightful home. Nor can you dismiss Tamas whom I appoint as Administrator.'

'You! You have no power.'

'I am the legitimate eldest daughter...'

'Don't expect me to believe my Grandfather made a deathbed marriage—illegal, in any case. I was the male heir and I inherit everything, and I am master here.'

'You may be under the delusion you are, but you are wrong,' and Irma gave a horrible triumphant smile.

It did not perturb Leonin in the least. He repeated, 'I am master here. I have already seen my grandfather's dead body in his bedchamber. Its being embalmed did not deceive me. I am now the Count Karpathy.'

'That is just what you are not,' retorted Irma. 'Because you committed treason against the Tsar, you have forfeited your civil rights in this country as well as in Russia. Tamas Szerb declares this to be the law.'

'An attainder prevents you from inheriting

213

Karpathy,' said the Administrator. 'Moreover three members of the Secret Police have come from Vienna to arrest you.'

'An arrangement made by Frau von Moricz, I presume.'

Valerie admired the way Leonin referred to their aunt by her surname as if rejecting any relationship. He spoke, she thought, as a nobleman should.

'The police agents have been summoned back to Vienna because of a fresh rising there. They left the village before Hugo I gather, so it astonishes me he did not inform you.'

'What business is it of yours what I did or did not tell my mother?' stormed the dissipated-looking Hugo. 'I have only just arrived at the Castle.'

'You have had sufficient time to impart that piece of news.'

'They would have arrested you and compelled you to go with them to Vienna.'

'That is something they would not have been able to do,' returned Leonin. 'I hold a written pardon from the Tsar of Russia proclaiming me guiltless of any treason. That secured my release from Siberia. So Tamas Szerb need not waste his breath in talking nonsense about attainders. I am the lawful Count Karpathy. As soon as my grandfather's remains have been put to rest in the family vault, the four of you are to leave this Castle. Go back to Miskolcz. It is only

214

through my gracious permission that you are allowed to stay until the funeral is over.'

Irma collapsed on the sofa behind which her mother still crouched. Irma was pale, but pallor did not diminish the expression of fury that showed plainly on her face. She had failed and she knew it. The two men also realised this, but Tamas Szerb glared maliciously, Hugo—whom Valerie decided was more drunk than she had guessed—giggled hilariously. He pointed a finger at her.

'And what about the cousin from England?'

Leonin answered haughtily, 'She will shortly become the Countess Karpathy, my wife.'

No comment was made concerning this announcement. Refreshments were served and eaten in silence. Aunt Irma retired, telling her son she was utterly worn out. Soon after, she left the room and he followed, and later Valerie heard from an elderly maid assigned to look after her that Herr Hugo had returned to the village. The same woman came to say a bedchamber had been prepared for Fraulein Gilliott. Valerie said goodnight to Leonin and he kissed her hand, explaining that he must learn what arrangements had been made for the funeral, and she realised he intended to question Tamas Szerb and take over preparations himself. Next day, Valerie heard the doctor and nurses from Debrecen had been sent back there.

The maid who waited upon Valerie was, like so many, a lifelong inmate of the Castle. She adored Leonin and shared in the general thankfulness for his return. It appeared that usually an interval of two weeks elapsed between death of a count and burial, but that was in order to allow time for relatives and other noblemen to make the journey. Leonin did not consider this necessary. He fixed the ceremony six days hence, and issued no invitations, only adhering to the custom of summoning extra clerics from Debrecen Cathedral. The village priest, Pater Josef, watched his dead lord's bier in the small chapel attached to the Castle. With due pomp the funeral took place and Valerie saw the grandfather she had never known lowered into the Karpathy vault. She still did not know whether or not he had learnt of her existence, or if her letter had been intercepted. Well, that did not matter now!

Leonin addressed his aunt as they emerged from the chapel.

'You and your party are to leave the Castle tomorrow morning. Such are my orders, and I shall insist on their fulfilment. If you do not go freely, you will be turned out.'

She shrugged her shoulders in acquiescence, while Hugo said sarcastically, 'Very well, Count. Oh, aren't you glad to have title and estate at last, though how you got round the

216

Tsar of Russia and managed to be freed from Siberia, beats me.'

Valerie could hardly believe that Leonin had achieved command so easily. She found it impossible to banish a feeling of terror that Aunt Irma roused in her, and during the last few days she was continually alone with time to brood over possible danger to her beloved. Yet all seemed to happen as it should.

Leonin apologised for the pressure of estate business that kept him from her, but he must learn all that had happened while Tamas Szerb held so many matters in his hands. The old Count had left a great deal to the Administrator in past months.

Valerie was glad that Hugo made no attempt to be friendly with her. In fact she hardly saw him. The weather was fine and he was supposed to be out on horseback, but she suspected him to be drinking heavily, also to be enjoying the society of his pregnant mistress. Aunt Irma did not go outside, so never went to the village and was apparently unaware that Kataya Strachan was staying at the inn. Valerie only hoped the aunt she had never liked and had now grown to hate was not plotting any revenge against Leonin. She told him of her fears, but he only laughed, assuring her he was safe among his faithful retainers.

With the funeral over, these people Valerie regarded as enemies would be leaving in less than twenty-four hours. Even the presence of Tamas Szerb was loathsome, although he was very humble and unobtrusive now. Still, she could not forget the way he behaved to her at Szolnok.

The Debrecen clerics had just departed, with the village priest, and Valerie lingered at the top of one of the hall staircases, hoping to see Leonin, but there was no sign of him. Instead she found herself followed by Tamas Szerb.

'The Count sent me Fraulein. He told me to enquire if you would like to see a portrait of your mother that he only discovered before the burial. No, it is not in the chapel. It has been removed to the late Count's bedchamber from an attic where he must have consigned it after the Countess Lilla's elopement.'

The room was quite near so Valerie, in spite of her mistrust of the man, had no misgivings about going that short distance with him. They reached the door which he opened, then stood aside for her to enter before he himself did so.

She had not noticed the heavy silk scarf tucked under his arm. Quickly he flung it round her face and arms, thus making it impossible for her to struggle, or even to cry for help.

CHAPTER TWELVE

Valerie struggled but was helpless in the vicelike grip of her captor.

He is as strong as he is evil was the thought which rushed through her mind as she endeavoured to use her only weapon, her nails, on his unpleasantly moist flesh, a characteristic that struck her when he had touched her cheek during their first meeting at the country fair. Aunt Irma was assisting Tamas Szerb now and she immobilised Valerie's hands while the girl was dragged along in silence. With covered mouth the prisoner could make no call for help.

Am I being taken somewhere to marry Hugo? Surely there is no benefit to Aunt Irma now in that ridiculous match.

Unless there was some plot to eliminate the new Count. Valerie shuddered. Since coming to Hungary she had feared for Leonin's safety. Yet it could not now be possible for their aunt to seize title and property, because Leonin was publicly in possession of Karpathy. As head of the family he had conducted the old Count's funeral.

Conscious of descending a steep staircase, then going along a bare floor which sloped downwards, and where she heard the ring of glass as one of her captors knocked something,

Valerie realised she was in the top wine cellar, the one still in use. After that she knew were a couple of empty ones, a flight of steps, then the final cavern where at one end was the grille giving secret access to the Castle.

Leonin had told her that he and his father were the only people aware of this grille since that part of the Castle was not only unused, but avoided because of its proximity to the Turkish tower. His words came back vividly and she could almost hear him explaining how the entrance had remained a secret.

'My father showed it to me and he said Grandfather showed it to him. None of the servants or the rest of the family knew of its existence.'

That was because none of them wished to go anywhere near the ancient tower or adjacent buildings. There was this belief in an imprisoned Turkish ruler's ghost that haunted the place. Valerie did not know that her grandfather had avoided it because he was really convinced the story was true, but Leonin's father was a thoroughgoing sceptic, and he took his son, determined the boy should not be superstitious, but be interested in the Castle's history.

Leonin had not told Valerie how frequently he did ramble in what he regarded as his special retreat. It had been a sudden impulse that caused him to confide in her about the secret entrance, and she was flattered he shared his secret with her. True it had crossed her mind that others might not be as superstitious as Leonin thought. She wondered especially about Tamas Szerb. As Administrator, surely he must be acquainted with every inch of the Castle, including the shunned part, unless he were afraid of the Turkish ruler's ghost. Of course he might be. As far as she knew he had never been as far as Pest. He might have legal qualifications, but he was a man of limited experience.

As for Aunt Irma, her mind was occupied with fulfilling her ambitions regarding Hugo. And Hugo—lazy and alcoholic!

She was certainly being taken to that region now. From her two previous visits she had a clear picture of it and was expecting any minute to be taken down the steps which led to a cellar, really like a cavern, and possibly, with grille removed, into the open air. Yes, Tamas Szerb must be familiar with that back way into the Castle. He might have discovered it during the years Leonin was away in Russia. Oh, where was Leonin? Pray God his life was not in danger. Pray God he would come to rescue her.

But no more steps were descended. Before reaching the point where the flight she expected began, Valerie found herself dragged to the left along what seemed to be a flat stone passage. She was then relinquished entirely to Aunt

221

Irma, whose grip was too firm for her to escape, or even to pull away the scarf wound round her face, neck and arms. Where on earth could she be?

Memory returned of the time Leonin brought her through the secret entrance in order to visit their grandfather's bedchamber and ascertain if the old man were really dead. With the grille pulled aside Leonin had helped her into the dark damp cavern, and together they climbed a long flight of steps where, at the top she now remembered, were two exits. They took one straight ahead, eventually reaching the inhabited part of the Castle. She recalled Leonin's lantern disclosing a side passage which, so he said, led to the Turkish tower. It was to that tower she was being taken by her captors.

They stopped. Tamas Szerb was in front and Valerie heard the sound of a key being inserted in a door. The Administrator had difficulty in turning it.

'Stiff from lack of use.'

'Oh, hurry up! Get the door open and help me push her inside. Then we can leave this horrible spot.'

Aunt Irma sounded extremely nervous. Valerie thought she was trembling.

'When were you last here, Tamas?'

'Two years ago, and that has been my only previous visit. It took great fortitude to explore the place. Inside the Tower is quite bare and there is no possibility of her escaping. Does your niece know how a tyrannical Turk was imprisoned and died here more than two hundred years ago? That was before the Turks were cleared out of our land. Yes, he starved to death as you will do, Fraulein. Not a nice end to one's life!'

'You will be locked inside and the key disposed of,' came Aunt Irma's harsh voice, for it was harsh and bitter with hatred. 'As for Leonin, Tamas and I will see he is also put out of the way. He shall not be an obstacle to my inheritance rights—rights I intend to pass to my Hugo, so that he becomes Count and Lord of Karpathy.'

Valerie had long ceased to struggle and the scarf prevented her from speaking. Besides, what could she say? Her own fate troubled her less than what might await Leonin. Despair for him overwhelmed her.

Tamas Szerb, still fiddling with a key in a lock, was boasting how brave he had been to make his previous visit. Then he proceeded to give details he had heard from Castle tradition concerning the prisoner who rotted away in this Tower, and how his ghost was known to haunt the place still. Nobody in the Castle or village, or even district, ventured here.

'As Administrator I felt it my duty to do so, but I own the prospect of meeting the spectre has not encouraged me to come again. I locked the door and retained the key. It shall be thrown in the river once you are secured inside, Fraulein Valerie.'

'Don't talk so much, Tamas! The ghost might appear.'

'He waits until dark they say.'

'Never mind! I want to quit this horrible part. I never came here as a girl, nor did anyone else, though I have heard my half-brother Julius did. But he was always odd.'

There was the sound of a heavy door creaking open. Valerie felt herself pushed inside, but on the threshold Tamas Szerb took hold of her and unwound the scarf wrapped around her. This 'freeing' as he called it gave him the chance to snatch a couple of kisses before Aunt Irma ordered him to make haste.

'Shut the door and lock it.'

'In a minute.' He ran his hand round her breasts.

Aunt Irma said with renewed impatience, 'Stop being a fool, Tamas. I brought you here to imprison the girl not make a fool of yourself over her. Shut and lock the door so that we can leave. When Hugo becomes Count I shall advise him to have the entire Tower blown up by gunpowder. My father once spoke of doing so, but that foolish Julius persuaded him to refrain.'

'Was Julius afraid of the Turk's ghost

224

exacting vengeance?' asked the Administrator, using any excuse for delay to fondle the nauseated Valerie.

'Julius refused to believe the legend, but he had mad ideas about undertaking explorations when he became Count. He used to say he was interested in some modern science called archaeology that uncovers secrets of the past. But stop dawdling, Tamas. You are sure Valerie cannot escape, aren't you?'

'There is no way out except through the door. The window slits in the wall are too high and much too narrow for even her to get through. Nor could she reach them.'

So Valerie discovered for herself when she was left alone. It was midday and the place lit by the sun gave light, but the so-called windows afforded no means of leaving the Tower.

Valerie's heart shrank as she looked at them, then at the closed heavy door which was, of course, locked. And her enemies had taken the key which was the only means of opening it. Nor was the door a wooden one that might be broken by heavy kicks.

I shall not see Leonin again, she thought gloomily. That was such an awful prospect that nothing else seemed to matter, not even the ghost of a long dead Turk. Not that she believed in the ghost. Leonin had not. Nor had his father, who must have been a strange, unusual man. Valerie pictured Uncle Julius coming to the Tower, curiosity overpowering fear, and he had influenced Leonin to be the same.

Leonin would never imagine that she, Valerie, would be imprisoned by his enemies here and left to face the long drawn out agony of hunger and thirst before death released her. If he were still free and had any notion where she was, he could not get into the place without the key. She might attract attention through the narrow windows if they could be enlarged, but she realised they were far too high for her to reach. Miserably Valerie struggled to her feet and began to walk round the Tower which consisted of the single great circular hall, perfectly rounded stone walls broken in the one place by a door locked against her. She had better make an inspection while light filtered through the windows, or openings as they were more appropriately termed. Without any real hope she began her pacing.

She was glad she had done so, for at the end furthest from the door she noticed loose stones in the floor. Yes, there was a break of about six feet square, and though this would only be obvious to anyone walking round looking for a break, she guessed it had never been noticed by Tamas Szerb on his single terrified visit to the Tower. Curious but terrified, he had probably only advanced a short way inside after opening the door to which he held the key, probably in private possession of the reigning Count Karpathy, and as Administrator Tamas had appropriated that possession during her grandfather's last year or so.

She began to pull at the loose stones. It was hard work and hurt her hands, but she was rewarded by making a gap large enough for her to squeeze through, only it led into utter darkness. She could see a little way down and distinguish rough footholes in what had been used by somebody getting out of the Tower, other than by the door.

As it could not have been the imprisoned Turk, might a later person have effected an entry that way? Had not Aunt Irma said to Tamas Szerb that Uncle Julius was such a sceptic he intended to explore this supposedly spectre haunted spot when Count? He might have done it before, thought Valerie, but would Leonin know about it? Would his father have taken him on any exploration when he was a boy? Of that she felt doubtful, but not that Uncle Julius had tried to penetrate the Tower from below, since the key to the door was in the late Count's possession—that is until Tamas Szerb managed to obtain it. Uncle Julius knew the secret of the grille entrance through cellars and how thus to get into the Castle itself, and today she, Valerie, had learnt that the door to the Tower was reached from the topmost wine cellar.

How much of the day was left? The sun would not set until late. Valerie curled up on the hard floor, close to the opening she had made, and tried to sleep, but she could not rest. She must get out of this Tower or die slowly of starvation. In desperation she began to feel her way down the footholes afforded by the opening. Never mind the darkness below! As for falling and breaking a limb, she dared not think of that possibility. She went on and on because she felt there was nothing else she could do. She must get free.

She lost all count of time, but at last she reached a flat expanse—yes, a floor. True it was hard and dusty, but it was a floor. She felt it. Then she realised that some way ahead was a glimmer of light. Moving stiffly forward, Valerie realised with joy that the light came from outside. She was in the cavern with the grille that when pulled aside would enable her to get into the open air.

She staggered along, struggling to keep going, and when at last she had emerged into the wood, she collapsed with relief on a patch of sun-drenched grass.

★   ★   ★

With his grandfather buried, Leonin watched the visiting clerics depart, thankful he could return to the immediate business of running the estate, which was now his. He had questioned Tamas Szerb on various matters before the funeral took place, and he had made no attempt to conceal his annoyance at the power possessed by the Administrator during the last year of the old Count's life.

He would be glad to see the man, with Aunt Irma and Hugo, leave the next day. He had no fears for his personal safety now he was publicly acknowledged as Count, for he was certain of the loyalty of household and villagers. It never occurred to him that revenge upon him might be achieved through the woman he loved.

Valerie was not in the library and Leonin was about to search for her in the garden when one of the footmen entered. This particular lackey looked somewhat flustered as he informed Count Karpathy that an unknown gentleman, and he hesitated at the word, was insisting on seeing His Lordship.

'He carries a pile of partly unrolled banners and a basket of tri-coloured cockades,' and by this strange description the footman tried to indicate why he had hesitated to admit him further than the hall.

'Good heavens, it is Kaspar!' Leonin stood up in delight and ordered this unusual visitor to be shown into his presence immediately.

There was an enthusiastic reunion of the two friends.

'I had decided not to stay any longer in

Szolnok nor ignore Karpathy on my way to Debrecen. Then I met Mother. She said she was coming to find me, having left the service of your aunt.'

'There was nothing further she could do here. Where is your mother now?'

'I left her at the village inn where she was bespeaking rooms for us.'

'My dear friend, you do nothing of the sort. You both stay here as my guests. I am the Count now. By the way, I must ask for your congratulations. Valerie has consented to be my wife.'

Kaspar responded with warm congratulations. Leonin summoned a lackey, ordering the man to find Miss Gilliott, convey his compliments, and request her to attend him in the library if she would be so kind.

'The three of us will drive to the inn and collect your mother. Meanwhile you can leave these banners and cockades here. You won't need them until you reach Debrecen, and that won't be for a week or so at least. I want to show you how I intend to be the model nobleman with due regard to the welfare and rights of his tenants and servants. Lajos Kossuth shall have no cause to complain of me. By the way, you received my gift, did you not? I refer to the jewels which are to be sold and the money received to swell the funds required by Kossuth for his struggle.'

Yes, Magda had handed them to her son, and he had arranged for their safe conveyance to the great leader. Kaspar thanked Leonin, though perhaps not so profusely as the gift demanded, but to Kaspar there was nothing over-generous, only much needed assistance for the freedom crusade. He was anxious to recruit Honveds from the Karpathy youth, but allowed Leonin to persuade him to defer this work for the present.

Leonin could not attend to Kaspar's eloquence about Honveds and such matters as he would once have done. His mind was too full of other things, including a desire to drive to the village and witness Valerie's reunion with Magda, for he realised the fondness between the two. He was disappointed when told that Fraulein Gilliott could not be found so must be somewhere in the Castle gardens. Rather than wait he left a message explaining his movements and drove off with Kaspar to fetch Magda and the Webbers' baggage.

He sensed an air of excitement even passing along the village main street, and certainly when alighting at the inn. Gabor met them with such a flow of Magyar as to be at first barely comprehensible.

'You are telling me that my cousin, Herr Hugo, has left and declared his intention of marrying the girl whom he brought to stay here? I cannot believe it.'

231

Magda appeared and supported the story.

'He and that girl Kataya Strachan, have just driven away, bound for Debrecen. He announced openly that he intended to marry her.'

'But he cannot do such a thing,' Leonin began indignantly, then stopped short. 'Not that it matters to me.'

'Frau von Moricz is your enemy,' said Magda.

'No, I no longer seek revenge. I merely want to get rid of her and her family, and all have been ordered to leave Karpathy tomorrow.'

'It is very noble of you, Count.'

'As soon as possible,' went on Leonin, 'I shall arrange with my cousin Valerie about our marriage. Yes, she has consented to accept me as her husband. Magda, you must come back to the Castle with me and Kaspar. In fact I need you until the marriage, for it is not fitting Valerie stays there without a chaperon.'

'Where is Fraulein Valerie?' asked Magda.

'At the Castle, of course. I meant to bring her with us to fetch you, but she could not be found. I think she was exploring the garden. We must hasten back and tell her the good news.'

'But Frau von Moricz?'

'She is at the Castle too, getting ready to leave tomorrow. Surely you do not mind meeting her. You left her service and she no longer can pretend to have authority over you. In fact it would not matter for her to know what your real purpose was in becoming her abigail. Her spying activities ended with loss of power to Metternich.'

'When she hears Herr Hugo has eloped with Kataya Strachan, she will be too overwhelmed to care about anything else,' said Magda solemnly. 'She has always been ambitious for him and this misalliance will break her heart.'

It was difficult to get away from the chatter at the inn, with Gabor and others expressing their opinions over the situation caused by this sensational elopement. Slight trouble with the carriage caused further delay, and Leonin grew impatient. He was perturbed lest Valerie should think him neglectful. Magda was anxious and said so.

'I feel worried in case Frau von Moricz and that wicked Administrator try to have their revenge upon you, Count.'

'What could they do now! I am beyond the power of their hatred.'

'Fraulein Gilliott might be at risk.'

'Whatever do you mean?'

'She could become a hostage. Through her they could hurt you.'

'Heavens, no!'

Leonin's face had lost every shred of colour. Kaspar, for once detached from his preoccupation with the Kossuth cause, tried to relieve any sense of impending tragedy by declaring his mother had been influenced by gipsies.

'We caught up with those old friends of yours, Leonin. You know, not the disreputable lot at Vienna, but the tribe we met at the fair, and you said they camped regularly near Karpathy—well, every spring. They are somewhere here now, having left Szolnok soon after you did. They said the old Count, your grandfather, allowed them to settle close to the Castle grounds.'

'My grandfather was a superstitious man,' declared Leonin. 'He was actually afraid of gipsies, just as he was afraid of the Turkish tower at one end of this Castle because it had the reputation of being haunted. Now my father was quite different. He trained me not to believe in such nonsense. Although I was only twelve when he died I continued friendship with those particular gipsies, and, as you know, Frau Webber, I have not avoided that part of the Castle attached to the Turkish tower. In fact, I secretly continued for years with the explorations my father had started there.'

'You must show them to Mother and me,' said Kaspar with somewhat forced politeness.

'Your mother knows the back way into the Castle. It is close to the Tower and, in fact, connected with it. I let Valerie and her into that secret when I smuggled her out before her journey to join you at Szolnok.'

He looked at Magda for confirmation and she gave a mechanical assent, but her mind was really elsewhere, and all three breathed a sigh of relief when the carriage reached the end of the drive and they were able to alight. Immediately they passed into the great hall, Leonin demanded from the footman who opened the front doors, where was Miss Gilliott?

'She cannot be found, My Lord. Every possible place has been searched but there is no trace of her.'

'What!'

The head footman, known as Groom of the chambers and clad in more resplendent livery than those under him, came forward to confirm this information. He had just given it to a now desperately worried Leonin when Aunt Irma appeared at the head of the grand staircase, followed by Tamas Szerb. Triumph shone on her face. She did not even notice her ex-abigail.

'You have deprived me and my son of our due inheritance, Leonin Karpathy. The law may be on your side but I have made it so that what you desire above title and estate is denied you. You are in love with Valerie Gilliott. Well, she will soon be dead. To all intents and purposes she is that already, and you can never rescue her.'

Leonin had rushed up to Irma and seized her, his face contorted with rage.

'You have abducted Valerie. Where is she? Tell me immediately.'

Laughter tinkled, an almost girlish laughter, while behind stood the Administrator, also smiling in derision.

'Guard them,' ordered Leonin.

A dozen servants had collected and surrounded the two enemies of their master.

'You shall not leave my Castle until you tell me where Valerie is.'

'I am only too delighted to inform you, nephew Count. She has been put in the Turkish tower. As you are aware, the only means of access is a heavy iron door, a door that cannot be broken down. Need I add that as Administrator, Tamas Szerb held the only key? After locking the door, he and I have been in the garden as far as the waterfall that discharges into the river. The key has been flung in there, so no human creature can reach Valerie, only the ghost of the old Turkish ruler! You will never see her again. She will of course starve to death. Not an enviable fate unless you kill her quickly by blowing up the tower with gunpowder. I seem to remember my father once saying he might do that. He hated the place, and his hatreds were certainly strong, just as he hated Lilla. Oh, he knew nothing about Lilla's daughter. Tamas intercepted the letter the foolish girl wrote and we saw no inkling of her existence ever reached him. It is unfortunate for you that she will not be available for you to wed, now his consent is not necessary.'

'I can get to Valerie,' Leonin whispered to Magda and Kaspar during his aunt's tirade.

'Can you really rescue her from that living tomb?' asked Magda incredulously.

The sound of her voice attracted Irma's attention. She poured out abuse against the abigail who had quitted her service.

'You can save your anger for your son, Frau von Moricz,' retorted Magda. 'Yes, I did take service in your household as a counter-spy to check on your spying for Prince Metternich. But my past activities will seem very unimportant when you learn what Herr Hugo has done.'

'I will soon tell her that,' remarked Leonin grimly. 'Hugo has gone to Debrecen with his pregnant mistress, Kataya Strachan. She was your abigail before Frau Webber. That pretty German girl you dismissed will now have become Hugo's legal wife, or soon will be. He set off with her an hour ago, having already made precise arrangements with one of the priests who attended Grandfather's funeral. The priest agreed to marry the couple. I wish you joy of your daughter-in-law, Madam. Of course we all know she is not of aristocratic lineage . . . '

But Leonin's remarks were drowned by violent shrieks from Irma. This was the final blow to ambitions long cherished for her son.

'You have given her a dreadful shock,' stormed Tamas Szerb. 'Her heart has always been weak,' he added, trying to reach Irma who had collapsed.

'She is dead,' said one of the footmen.

Leonin took no notice. He could feel no grief for a woman who had behaved to both himself and his beloved with such fiendish cruelty. He ordered her body to be taken to her bedchamber, for the village physician to be summoned, while the former Administrator was to be kept prisoner.

'For you I shall call in a law authority from Pest. I want the utmost penalty exacted from you for your attempted murder of Miss Gilliott.'

'Do what you like with me,' screamed Tamas Szerb who had not heard what Leonin had said to his friends about the possibility of gaining access to the Tower. 'The woman you love is as good as dead. You wanted her for your wife but that she can never be.'

Leonin did not deign to contradict Tamas Szerb. He said to Magda and Kaspar, 'Follow me', and while the servants stared in amazement, he strode through the hall and down to the kitchen quarters, then through the cellars. The hole where Valerie had managed to loosen sufficient loose stones to get through was obvious from below. So was the fact that the grille was open.

Scrambling through it Leonin saw a group of his gipsy friends, including their leader who came towards him.

'The lady, Ban, she has fainted, but she is breathing all right. Her hands are bleeding. She must have been handling rough stones. She needs to be put to bed and given nourishing soup.'

Thus when Valerie recovered consciousness, her first reaction was to the warm comfort of freshly laundered sheets. Her hands were sore. She felt bandages round them. Then she heard strains of soft music. Someone was playing a lilting tune on a curious instrument, as though gentle little hammers were being struck.

Raising herself on the pillows, she met the eyes of her beloved, her cousin Leonin whom she had first seen at Baron Beckmann's party in Vienna. Then he was disguised as a gipsy and taking part in an orchestra hired to entertain the guests.

Leonin put aside the czimbalom and hungrily took her in his arms. The horror of imprisonment in the Turkish tower seemed like a stark nightmare from which she had awakened to blissful freedom, to a state of perfect happiness because she was with Leonin and knew beyond doubt that he loved her. This was no mirage like the fairy world of Fata Morgana, but reality.

As in a trance she listened to him saying again and again, 'Thank God, you are safe, my darling!'

Photoset, printed and bound in Great Britain by REDWOOD PRESS LIMITED, Melksham, Wiltshire
240